INTO THE WOOD

A VIC SHAPESHIFTER COLLECTION

By Yvonne Rediger

Dedication

For the readers, you make this all possible.

Miss Agnes and the Garry Oaks

Agnes Esme stooped and picked another mushroom to add to her half-filled basket.

You had to be careful to pick the right mushrooms, not all were edible. Some would give you a stomach ache, some would make you sleep until next week enduring nightmares, and some, well, those ones took you off this planet and left your relatives with a bill from the undertaker.

It was an exceedingly good thing Agnes knew which mushroom types fell into which category. Today, she was picking the eating kind.

Agnes straightened slowly. Her poor old back didn't like all the bending and stretching. Still, she would be damned if she'd lay down on the ground to pick mushrooms like Kath Sealy had when her back finally couldn't take the bending over anymore. There was no point in risking the pneumonia even if this was a very warm spring day and the yellow prairie violets were blooming with their first flowers.

She shaded her eyes as she scanned the immediate vicinity looking for more wild mushrooms to pick. That's when she spied William Fellows striding down the narrow curving path. He was coming her way.

The old woman wrinkled her long thin nose in distaste at the middle-aged balding man. William Fellows was a silly boy with a wee bit of power.

She drew her tatty grey sweater around her and buttoned the two remaining buttons like a sniper checking the rounds in his rifle. She knew what was coming.

"Miss Agnes!" William called out, waving at her.

She snorted. Like she couldn't see him approaching.

"Meh." Agnes turned away.

She made her way carefully over to the shade of a large Garry oak tree. She placed her feet just so, to avoid crushing the blooming flowers. The tree's wide trunk was blanketed in vibrant green moss. There were three choice mushrooms peeking out among the tall strands of young grass, attached to a decaying log. Agnes snatched them up and dropped them into her basket.

"Miss Agnes, you really shouldn't be on this side of the fence." William Fellows voice chided, sounding more than a bit patronizing.

Again Agnes slowly straightened. Standing tall, she turned to face the Garry Oaks Preserve supervisor. She narrowed her gaze on him, using her second best steely glare.

"Billy Fellows, don't you take that tone with me," she warned.

Immediately, William's face changed. He returned to a ten year old boy who had been caught stealing Macintosh apples from Miss Agnes' orchard over forty years ago.

"I'm sorry Miss Agnes, but the Preserve isn't open to the public, you know that. You shouldn't be in here walking around the grounds. You aren't even a registered volunteer." William struggled to meet the old woman's eyes.

Miss Agnes' steely gaze was just one of the things that made kids think Agnes Esme was a witch. Those kids were right. Children can sometimes sense important things that adults have completely dismissed, or told themselves not to be silly, the old lady was harmless. No so much.

She could see William valiantly struggle past the old superstitions. It was evident he was trying to think of Miss Agnes as just a regular old busy body who thought her age allowed her to flout the rules. Agnes's manner made that difficult.

"Aah!" Agnes scoffed, deep enough to almost spit. "I don't need to be a registered volunteer of the Preserve to tend the plants here. I know my horticulture Billy, and I've been harvesting mushrooms and other plants from this land, which used to be *my* land." Agnes ladled a thick serving of sarcasm on the last words. "Well before you were a gleam in your mother's eye."

Then Agnes focused even harder on William and gave him the look that everyone dreaded. Agnes locked one filmy eye on him and asked in a menacing tone, "Or are you questioning my competence?"

"No, no, Miss Agnes." William could feel himself wilt under her regard. "I know, you know your stuff, it's just that the rules are the same for everyone. If people see you in here, others will think they can jump the fence too. The next thing you know, this land will be overrun with," William said with a shudder. "Dog people."

They both curled their lips at that thought and shared a grimace.

"They don't always clean up after their pets and some just bag it, to toss it in the bushes. I'm sure you've seen what has happened on the sea walks."

"I am not *everyone*, Billy." Agnes said derisively. "The dog people won't dare let their animals defecate on my land." Her tone spoke of dire consequences for irresponsible dog owners.

Despite her words, Agnes liked animals of every stripe, however not necessarily the people that came along with them.

William knew this was a losing battle. The rest of the volunteers had given up trying to convince Agnes Esme that she should confine herself to the walkway and the lookout platform. Most stopped trying to deter her from wandering the Preserve. That was, except for when their organization hosted an open house for the public. Even so he was still determined to give it one last try.

"May I point out that it isn't your land anymore Miss Agnes, you sold it to the municipality years ago."

"I sold the land, not the rights to the plants. Are you trying to deny me my historical rights?" She raised one shaggy black eyebrow at him.

"Um, no, I guess not," William said, he conceded with a shiver.

"What exactly am I doing that is disturbing you?" Agnes asked in an almost reasonable tone.

William stared at her for a long moment, should he tell her?

"It's not the mushroom picking, Miss Agnes. We have a dead patch of trees and we are trying to determine the cause of the blight. We're worried it might spread to the other trees."

"What! Why didn't you say so, boy? Take me there immediately." Miss Agnes strode down the path the way she had come.

William was forced to jog to keep up with the old woman as he wondered how she knew which direction to go.

It wasn't more than a five minute walk. Or rather jog, to arrive at the ring of dead grass and charred remains of several two hundred year old oaks.

"Someone tried to do a burning here, and failed miserably." Miss Agnes gripped the basket handle until her knuckles went white and she got a handle on her anger. Her heart ached for the lost trees.

"That was our guess too." William agreed panting.

"It's too early in the season to do a prescribed burn." Miss Agnes commented as she surveyed the fourteen foot blackened circle.

Agnes breathed in and caught the smoke and charred greenery smell, not what she was looking for. She closed her eyes and sifted through the various scents, sorting the fresh green and flowery scents from the charred wood stink. There it was. The one thing she had feared, the taint of malice, evil, and malevolence.

This was no attempt at a prescribed burn. This destruction had been done with a different intention.

Agnes hid her thoughts as she opened her eyes and cut them to William. "Where is Matthew Elkhorn?"

"He's on his way. I called him first thing." William confirmed he had notified the authorities.

"Good," Agnes grunted. "Let me know what he finds, better yet, tell him to come get me when he's done with his investigation and we will see what we can do for these oaks."

William sighed in resignation. "Yes, Miss Agnes."

The old woman nodded and turned away to walk back through the oaks to her own garden gate.

Ten minutes later, Agnes lifted the latch and effortlessly swung the portal open and then closed it again behind her. She paused only a moment, and looked over her shoulder at the gate. This was to ensure the entrance settled back into the surrounding cedar fence snugly. Then the gate transformed back into being, for all appearances, a large bush of spiny blackberries.

Blackberry bushes had unique properties for protection of property. However, you had to make sure their borders were well defined. The plant liked to spread out and see how far it could go before anyone noticed.

Agnes rounded the side of her white clapboard house, and deposited her basket in the shade of the front porch beside her wooden rocking chair. She would take the contents to barter later, once she did a perimeter check.

Pushing up the sleeves of her sweater to expose thin, boney arms, Agnes headed for the garden gnomes. The small statues were positioned in humorous poses among the flower beds that lined the front garden.

There were digging gnomes, raking gnomes, some holding up baskets of painted flowers, hedge clipper gnomes, waving gnomes, and each type had both boy and girl. All were brightly painted with smiling happy faces as they went about their chores.

The most recent addition, a football playing gnome had been given to Agnes as payment for sorting out a neighbor's problem with their composter and raccoons.

Agnes particularly liked the new wee green man. He was burly but slimmer than the rest of the garden gnomes and seemed to be in better physical shape. These football gnomes were worth looking into as future additions to beef up the protection grid.

Taking a soft cloth from her pocket, she employed it to clean off any dust or pollen that coated each of the gnomes pointed hats, coats and faces.

As she worked, Agnes checked the bindings each gnome held. When she got near the hedge clipping gnomes, the binding felt disturbed and there was a definite gap. There was a break in the working of the wards since the last time she had checked them.

Dread crawled up Agnes' spine.

Something had definitely gotten out...

Author's note: To find out what happens next, read Hell Cat, book 2 in the VIC Shapeshifter series.

The Wolf of Crofton Lake

Courtney Tremblay walked quickly up Robert Street, with only a distant street light to illuminate her way. The night was heavy and humid, which was unusual for it being this close to fall.

A gentle late summer breeze escaped from the thick wall of trees to caress her tanned face with the scent of maple leaves turning and arbutus bark peeling. There was also the scent of water from the small stream, the last wild flowers, and her own perspiration from the laborious walk.

She glanced over her shoulder and down the dimly lit street. The town was quiet and still, and as far as she could tell, no one was following her.

This wasn't reassuring.

Courtney couldn't shake the feeling she wasn't alone. She blew out the breath she'd been holding, and dismissed the feeling as she trudged uphill to the top of Robert Street. She arrived at the head of the forest trail which stretched out behind the town's water facility. The trail would take her home.

It was well past one o'clock in the morning, but she knew her grandmother would still be up, and prowling the front porch waiting for her. That thought made her cringe, partly with guilt for worrying her family, and partly for the tongue lashing she was in for. Not that she didn't deserve it, usually, but this time it wasn't all her fault.

Maybe it was unusual for most nineteen-year-olds to have a curfew, but not for the girls in Courtney Tremblay's family. The curfew was applied to the boys too, everyone was home before midnight. That curfew had come and gone more than an hour ago. She'd been annoyed to find and her ride had left without her. She'd been having too much fun, now she regretted the last beer on the beach by the fire.

The small hairs on the back of her blonde head prickled. Courtney paused in the shadow of an enormous arbutus tree which marked the boundary of the Village of Crofton and the trail head that led to Crofton Lake. Again she listened hard, but heard nothing other than the slight stirring of leaves. Someone was out there, she was certain of it. They were being careful not to be heard or seen.

As soon as Courtney had left her friends, and away from the beach, she'd sensed it. Even though she couldn't pick up anything to prove to the primitive part of her brain who might be following her.

Her grandmother's words came to her. "If you sense something isn't right, it probably isn't. Trust your instincts. They've kept us alive for thousands of years."

Courtney breathed in and out deeply to slow down her heart rate. She compressed her lips into a straight line as she promised herself she would have words with her cousin Mark tomorrow for leaving her behind. He'd put her in this predicament. But right now, she had to focus on getting home on her own.

She scooped up her loose, long dark blonde hair and let it flow over her shoulder as she did yet another quick check behind her.

Again, nothing.

Unease wrapped a thin tendril around her spine at not being able to identify the source of her apprehension. She shook herself as though to dislodge the feeling and continued on, though the feeling of being stalked did not lessen as she strode down the uneven trail.

Tonight had been her last chance to say goodbye to her friends. While her fellow high school grads thought it was exciting to be going to university in Vancouver, Courtney wasn't as sure. She loved the Island, with her family and friends around her. Okay maybe jobs were scarce, but that didn't matter. She loved horticulture and organics, so a degree in agriculture and land economics appealed to her, and would have meant university in any case.

Courtney was willing to do whatever it took to be able to come home to work when she had her degree. The Island was where her heart lie.

Now wasn't the time to think about that, she needed to pick up her pace.

Courtney passed the last of the village's water reservoir tanks and took the path that led deeper into the forest. It also led up the back side of Mount Richards and the farm.

She would risk the shorter route. It meant the sliver of the last August moon would do little to brighten the trail that Courtney's flat heeled sandals navigated. Even so, it was only a little over two kilometres to her grandmother's backdoor. Piece of cake.

The pungent forest scents teased her nose as she strode down the path. She wished the wind was coming from the opposite direction.

Along with the types of trees, she could pick out the lingering roses and other wild flowers as well as the ubiquitous ferns. Listening intently, Courtney headed down the trail, further from Crofton and closer to home. Unfortunately, she couldn't identify anything that didn't belong.

Courtney's grandfather had taken her on this walk between their farm and Crofton, first when she was three years old. Since then she must have traveled the route hundreds of times in the past sixteen years, although rarely at night and never by herself. Such were the rules.

There was a faint snap of a twig a good distance behind her, causing Courtney to spin around. Her long hair flung out from her shoulders as goose bumps sprang up on her bare arms and legs. She held stock still for a moment and listened intently, not even breathing.

A fluttering sound made Courtney frown. It could be an owl that made the noise, as it dove for a rabbit or mouse, hunting for its supper she told herself. She stared behind her into the darkness, but saw nothing.

Turning around again, she carefully placed one foot in front of the other, as quietly as possible. She was good at being quiet in the wood–she'd had lots of practice. The careful steps reminded her of the story she would beg her grandpa for each time they walked the path, when she was younger. His wrinkled face would fold into a smile, and he would give in to her pleas with a gentle squeeze to the small hand he held in his.

"The Wolf of Crofton Lake," was how he would begin. And Courtney would shiver with anticipation. She'd hung on every word as they walked down the slight incline in the trail. The track led to the south end of the small man-made lake.

Courtney remembered the exact cadence of her grandpa's voice as she took the same route in the shadows of the giant trees.

Aloud, she whispered the story to herself. They were comforting and familiar. She imitated her grandfather's rhythm as she spoke the words under her breath.

"Many people heard the cry of a wolf ripple across the dark water. Some said he sounded angry. Some said he sounded lonely, and others said it was too frightening to go down to the lake at night to find out." She would never interrupt the flow of the story. She didn't want to break the spell.

The smell of marsh and open water became ever more distinct as she travelled down the trail. The access road merged with the trail that bordered the bottom end of the lake and ran out to Osbourne Bay Road.

"Some thought they had seen the shape of the huge wolf in the shadows as he prowled the lake shore looking for his prey. Some said he wasn't looking for prey at all. Food was easy to come by for the cunning hunter, and the evidence was sometimes left as a warning on the lake's shore."

Courtney stepped over a fallen log.

"Was he calling for his mate? Howling his grief, others wondered? Why did his mate not answer his cry? Could the she-wolf have been killed by the lumberjacks? The men would take on any challenge but feared the wolves would attack them unawares. The workers were vulnerable when their backs were bent, sawing the old growth trees by hand. So the lumberjacks killed any wolf they saw first before–," she broke off at the distinctive sound of footsteps. He was growing bolder.

This time Courtney stepped off the trail and hid behind a four hundred year old cedar. The massive girth of the tree shielded her from the trail and she waited, heart pounding. She struggled to remain still. Her feet wanted to run.

The wind shifted, now coming from behind Courtney. A break in the trees allowed a sliver of moonlight to outline a man-sized shape to steel cautiously down the trail and pause only few feet away.

"Don't be afraid," his rough voice was pitched to carry down the trail. "I saw you come in here, and I was worried you'd lose your way in the dark. I can help you." He spoke like a man trying to coax a skittish animal to his hand, while he hid a weapon.

"I don't need help, thank you," Courtney said tipping her head up as she spoke so her voice would be lost among the trees.

She watched him glance around the clearing, trying to locate her. He didn't know where she hid.

The man was much larger than Courtney, and she didn't recognize him. He was old, looked to be in his forties. An odd, rank odour, emanated from him. Like the smell of old deer entrails and curdled dried blood.

"Come out so I can see you're all right." He had long dark hair pulled back into a greasy ponytail and his posture was slightly hunched over. He wore a long coat which was unusual for the hot weather. One pale, skinny hand and wrist was exposed, as he opened and closed it into a fist. It seemed to be a nervous tick. The other hand was buried deep in his coat pocket, but most frightening of all, was the glittering hunger reflected in his black eyes.

"You'll just have to take my word for it." Courtney was getting annoyed and forgot to tip her head up as she spoke to disguise her location. His shiny eyes locked on to her even though she had been sure he couldn't see her.

He moved slowly toward her hiding spot and squinted into the gloom. "Come out where I can see you."

"Why? So you can grab me? I don't think so." Courtney sidled to the left and slid between the trees and a branch snapped.

"I want to help you," he said again in a breathy tone as he neared her.

Courtney slipped away, deeper into the natural tree cover, but her flat shoes weren't made for traversing the underbrush, and she slipped and stumbled. She knew she was making too much noise and that the man could track her. She felt her heart constrict with fear as she moved faster, not bothering with trying to be quiet now.

He zeroed in on her, moving fast. He was only a few feet behind when he lunged, and tried to grab her arm. He got too close, and his long fingernails caught at her, scratching her skin.

"Leave me alone!" She screamed as she looked for a likely tree to climb or hide behind as she ran further into the dark wood. But there was no time with her pursuer on her heels.

"I won't hurt you," he cried as he went after her, but his actions belied his words.

He was too fast and Courtney felt tears gather as she ran, her breath was coming in gasps and she could feel her control starting to give way. She ran harder, right out of her sandals and then dodged left into some brush.

She pulled her shirt over her head and let her other-self take hold. Her true-self flowed through her system like a flooding river rushing into a still lake.

The change encompassed the human Courtney and shifted her into a lean, sleek brown wolf with glowing amber eyes. The she-wolf shook off the shredded clothing and slipped soundlessly through the trees, then circled around behind the man.

"Come out, and I'll drive you home," he panted. His head was moving from side to side.

No doubt trying to locate her again. She watched through narrowed eyes as he scanned the wood for her. His hand was out of his pocket now. Sharpened steel glinted in the moonlight as the man convulsively gripped the handle of an axe.

Making her decision, the wolf leapt. She hit the man's back and her strength drove him to the ground with a muffled thud. The impact caused the axe to tumble out of his hand.

Claws dug painfully through the dirty canvas coat as the wolf released a low growl. Terror overcame the man—he couldn't speak or scream for help.

All he could manage were guttural noises as fear closed his throat and the off-spring of the Wolf of Crofton Lake closed her jaws on the back of his neck.

Author's Note: This story happens before Magic's Price, book 4.

Finding the Wolf

He still couldn't remember his own name. Was this part of becoming a shapeshifter? His old identity wiped away? He wasn't sure how he felt about the situation, but was more concerned with survival.

His fingernails scraped frantically against the cold stone as he fell. The impact on the rocks shocked the breath from his lungs. Body bruised and aching, he climbed to his feet. Again, he plunged bleeding hands into jagged cracks in the split rock for handholds. Bare feet braced against the mountain side, he heaved his human shape upward. The stone was ice-cold and slippery from past snowfalls. It complicated his struggle to get off the sandstone ledge.

The wind numbed him all over as he inched upward for the sixth time. It made him clumsy as he quashed thoughts of hypothermia. There was nothing he could do about his lack of clothing right now anyway.

A slice of moon stabbed the clear star-studded night sky. It did little to illuminate the side of the mountain or show him a better route back up to the trail. Muscles bunched and shaking with effort, he found a handhold to gain another six inches. This was farther than he'd gotten before. A spark of hope warmed him.

His predator eyes might show him a way out, and he was stronger in his other shape, but Wolf couldn't climb. Then too, there was the problem of changing shape. He couldn't remember how, not fully. A problem he'd deal with once back up on the trail. Shifting would be the only way he'd survived this frigid night.

He found a tree root to grab, and with the other hand, he patted the rock. Where was the next handhold?

Nothing. It was all smooth rock face.

His arms trembled as he changed hands and reached out with his right. Dirt trickled over his fist clenched around the root. A bad omen.

Abruptly, the root pulled out of the thin soil. He slammed against the rock again, his vision going dark. Frustration and anger made the panic rise. Stay in control. He struggled to inhale and tramp down the fear. If he let the fear rule him, he could not think, and then he'd die.

A disjointed memory surfaced in his discouraged mind. A comforting hand brushed his face, the touch easing some past trauma. The gentle fingers ignited a flow of energy in his body, erasing the pain.

"Come on," she whispered to him. She smelled wonderful, her scent made him think of the wide-open prairie. How the sun warmed the land, releasing its wild fragrance.

He blinked and looked up at her. Bright blue eyes sparked back, filled with a mother's love. "You can do it." He knew she said it, but the words were not from her lips. "Here we go." Like water flowing down hill, he'd changed into Wolf.

A being stronger, so much more alive. Fear was gone, pain was gone.

The old woman smiled down at him. "Good." Then she made him change again, and sleep.

The next time he awoke, a young female occupied the hospital bed six feet away from his.

Her arms were strapped down on either side of a muscle-hard body. Her ankles too, were bound to the corners of the frame.

A dark head turned his way, she must have sensed he was awake. Dark brown eyes looked at him with pure hate. She lifted her lip at him, despising him.

He swallowed and looked away. The old woman was gone, but their captor was back. Sybil, was her name. She came to his bedside. He remembered how she'd twisted and tore at the energy within him. She tried to make him change, but he'd never done it, not for her. Only for the old woman.

His voice was still rough from pleading with Sybil to stop. But she was mad. He could smell it on her and see the crazy in her eyes.

"You did it for her, you can do it for me." She pierced him with needles of energy.

Panic, his old friend was back.

The mad woman triggered the change, and the situation changed too.

Wolf was free from the restraints. The huge animal leapt from the bed and made a dash for the door.

He stopped. This wasn't right. Turning swiftly, the wolf darted back, knocking Sybil aside. His teeth grabbed the leather strap of restraint on her right hand.

Wolf bit cleanly through. His tongue and the inside of his mouth burned, but she was free.

The female changed into a huge wolf and lunged right for the mad woman.

"No, no, you should love me," Sybil cried as she tried to fight off the wolf. The scuffle knocked medical equipment over. A light fell and landed on a bed. Immediately the sheets caught fire.

Fear washed through him. The flames were between Wolf and the door.

He dove for a window and knocked it out of the frame before falling to the floor. In the distance he heard the glass smash as it hit the ground. He got his paws under him. The room was filling with smoke. The flames dashed up the cloth dividers.

There was the snap of a neck. The smell of death.

Wolf turned to see the rabid female drop the limp human body to the floor.

The she-wolf snarled and charged. He froze. She leapt over him and out the window. Not knowing what else to do, he followed.

One behind the other, they ran past other people mesmerized by the fire. There was an explosion. They kept running, heading for the mountains. An hour after their escape, the female turned. He came to an uncertain stop on the trail.

Her yellowed-eyed glare should have warned him. She went for his throat, he was sure he'd die.

The female was clumsy and only succeeded in knocking him over a cliff with the force of her attack.

He woke sometime later, frozen and alone.

One bloody and dirty hand grasped a new tree root. This one was stronger. He hauled his body up another foot. He frowned. Being knocked unconscious must have triggered his change back to human shape. Was that how this worked?

His hand fit into a crack in the rock. He let go of his root hold too soon, the sandstone crumbed in his left hand. He went limp as he fell again, but kept his head up. Maybe he'd learned something.

Gingerly, he climbed to his feet. Everything ached. The pungent scent of a small animal drifted on a cold breeze. His stomach growled.

Once again he looked up at the daunting climb, and then down at his abused, bleeding hands. He turned his back on the challenge and touched his forehead. The blood was dry and the cut from his head impacting the rock earlier, almost healed. He examined his hands and watched the wounds close. Freaky as hell.

He looked down.

He should be dead the same as the mad woman.

His head began to ache he sighed at the new pain.

Looking down, he could see scrub and rocks along the mountain side. Even in the dark, he sensed a narrow valley open below him.

How high up was he? Would it be easier to climb down than back up to the mountain? The she-wolf was up there, and he wasn't anxious to find the female. Hate rolled off of her in waves.

He knew that Sybil woman had done something to him. But it was the older one who made him feel whole again.

What had the older female triggered? He touched his chest, under his heart. Closed his eyes, searching for the feeling she evoked. Could he trigger the change? Should he?

There, the pool of deep energy she'd shown him. How did it work?

The temperature was dropping, the crisp air promised snow, and his breath formed a cloud as he released it. With a shiver he glanced down the slope, it was looking better all the time.

He straightened away from the stone and spread his feet for stability. If he could remember how he shifted to the wolf, chances were good he could get out of here. After that, well, he would look for food, and then who knew?

One step at a time, stay alive.

He reached inside himself again, and visualized the indigo pool of energy. This time he reached for it. A warm, clean sensation washed over him. Was it this easy he wondered? Willingly he felt the change take him, it was almost painless.

Blinking in surprise, Wolf stood on four large paws. He stretched, and then lifted his head to scent the air. One smell he immediately identified as food.

Through narrowed eyes, he scanned the shadowy slope. There was a game trail down the side of the mountain to the valley floor.

Sounds traveled to him, he could track the movement of creatures below him. It was nothing to turn toward the edge of the cliff and jumped down. He knew exactly where to put his feet as he trotted downhill. It didn't matter how steep the grade.

Wolf did not feel fear that was for the human side. As he slowed to walk down the incline he decided the small creature to the left would be his meal. He did not name it, the animal was merely prey and barely a mouthful. He must do better.

Wolf slipped between the bushes satisfied he was on level ground again. With a slow turn to the left, he targeted his prey. Head level and unmoving, he inched closer, approaching from down-wind. Another prey, unaware, paused to swipe at its whiskers and long ears. Wolf's hindquarters gathered under him. He coiled his muscular legs in preparation to spring.

The Call hit him sharply in the chest. It did not frighten him, but the strength caught him by surprise. It wasn't a sound, but pure energy, and familiar. It tugged at his power and made him want to answer.

Still, he froze as it touched him and stroked over his long body. The touch did not make him cringe. It was familiar.

His prey sniffed the air. Wolf's attention was drawn back to it. The prey shot though the scrub and was gone. He'd been detected. Slowly, Wolf straightens out of his crouch, his still empty stomach never felt more hollow.

The Call came again, stronger this time, and felt like a homing beacon. It pulled at him, getting under his skin. Wolf turned and looked down the throat of the gully. Tiny flakes of snow began to drift out of the dark sky as he moved north.

The irresistible pull of the Call rippled through him again. Wolf could not stop himself from heading toward it. First walking, then loping, and finally dashing as fast as he could toward the appeal.

Much to Wolf's irritation, what was left of him and resided in a tiny corner of Wolf's mind, finally woke.

"How do we know it's not the ones we ran from?" He questioned the wolf's decision to travel toward the summons.

Wolf did not know for sure, but it felt right. Safe, he suggested. Even so, he slowed to a trot as the stone curved again. The farther he traveled, the colder the valley grew as the wind picked up and hit him in the face. Wolf progressed along the rocky ground and it grew coated in slippery snow. He employed his claws to keep his footing and left large tracks behind him.

The gully turned into a canyon with curving walls rising up on either side of him. Wolf slowed to a cautious walk, not liking the closed in feel as the walls rose higher. The valley changed direction and the wind shifted around, now blowing from behind him. The barrier restricted his sight and he could not smell what was ahead.

"I don't like it." Wolf felt his human fear rising.

He curled his lip.

"We could be in danger."

Wolf ignored him and his fear. The closer he got to the Call, the more right it felt. The sides of the canyon branched off to the right and the wolf pace slowed as he rounded the curve. He scanned the area for threats.

Then he saw it, a small figure with arms reaching high overhead. Palms open and holding an iridescent globe of indigo-blue light. The illumination shot straight up, bright and sharp, like a star before falling down into sparks in a drifting pattern, mixing with the falling snow.

Wolf stopped and stared.

He watched the display with him, looking out through the wolf's eyes too. They registered the source of the light was human shaped and female, but more.

"Is it her?" He asked Wolf. But Wolf did not respond as he sampled the air, tasting something familiar.

The clothing she was wrapped in only left a small part of her face visible. Then the blue light vanished. The female slowly lowered her arms to her sides. Her eyes locked on Wolf's in an exchange he could not break.

"Don't be afraid," the female said. Her voice was familiar too. "We're here to help you."

A second female stepped away from the rock wall. This one was different from the tiny one. Her stance spoke of strength and confidence. By her intelligent eyes, Wolf recognized one of his own.

Alpha, Wolf thought as he gazed at her.

"It's all right, we have food for you," the tiny one said and turned away for a moment. The aroma of raw meat hit the air and involuntarily Wolf moved forward, drawn within six feet of the pair. Moisture filled his mouth, his eyes now focused on the red meat.

"Here," the tiny one said and tossed him the cut of beef.

Wolf lunged forward, and snatched the meat out of the air. He devoured it in fast, large bites than looked up at the female for more. While he'd eaten the first piece, the tiny one had moved closer and now offered a second chunk of meat. He took this one too and ate it just as fast.

"Good thing we brought lots of steaks," the alpha said.

"Yes, you were correct in your guess he couldn't pass up the food." The tiny one smiled.

"It's her," he said, as Wolf chewed the final bite. He stayed where he was, allowing the tiny one touch him.

Energy flowed through him, making him freeze in place. The world slipped side-ways and the next thing he knew, he was sitting buck naked in the snow, in his human form. He blinked stupidly up at the females.

"Hello Christopher, are you ready to go hunting? We have a female shapeshifter to find." The alpha studied him with glowing amber eyes.

Monster Makeup

"This is ridiculous. I look fluffy," Travis Cowidgin said. The First Nations youth glared at his reflection in the light-framed mirror. "I'm supposed to be a scary werewolf."

"I'm not finished." Paige St. Claire turned the swivel chair to her right with the help of her knee. "Stop moving." She leaned in and brushed luminous green makeup down the left curve of Travis' nose. "Making scary monsters is my specialty."

He shifted restlessly again and this time Paige allowed a growl to emanate from her throat. The kid stilled. She nudged the chair again to access Travis' cheekbone. Deftly, she curved the brush over his skin to make his bone structure stand out.

"I don't look anything like my half-form." Travis managed to not move his face this time when he spoke.

"No, you're not supposed to." She lifted her palette of paints to reload the brush. "I have my instructions, and this is what the director wants." Paige frowned at the drawing on the yellow-lined paper she'd taped beside the mirror. "I wonder if Andre took into account the colour of the paper he used."

"What? Are you saying this all might be wrong?" Travis' voice rose slightly. "I've been sitting here for two hours."

"Settle Travis, it'll be fine." Paige added a stroke of colour down the other side of his nose to match the first. The additional paint made his snout-shaped nose stand out. "The director has his vision." She stood back and looked at the result of her painstaking work. "This should do."

Travis swivelled the chair back to the mirror once again. "I look stupid." His tone was sulky as only an eighteen-year-old's voice could be. He turned his eyes up to Paige, the contact lenses made them red instead of their usual dark-brown. "Why can't I just use my own shapeshifter half-form? For real?"

"Because I doubt your half-form is scary enough for film. Besides, the alphas would have my hide as well as yours. No one is supposed to know there are shapeshifters on Vancouver Island."

"Couldn't you just put makeup on my half-form face? In warrior shape I really am pretty scary."

Her lips twitched, wanting to smile. "I'm sure you are, but what if someone figured out you and Mindy actually are shapeshifters? What if they ran away screaming to the authorizes? Then what?"

He folded his arms over his chest. "This sucks."

"Don't wrinkle your costume." She gestured for him to drop his arms. "Look on the bright side. You're getting paid to be in an Andre Mortimore film. You even have a few lines." She picked up a cloth from the makeup table and began cleaning her brushes. "How many people get to be in a movie, even once in their lives? Suck it up, Buttercup."

"I could tell Andre some of us are shapeshifters, if anyone would understand it's him. If we were in California and part of that other pack, we would. I should show him what I really look like, then the movie would be more realistic, and more like the truth."

Paige laughed ruefully at his remark. "Who said anything about wanting the truth? This is a monster movie, nobody wants the truth. People just want to be entertained." She pulled off her latex gloves. "Now, stand up and I'll take some photos of you." She shoved her blonde ponytail over her shoulder and stuck a hand into the pocket of her paint-stained smock for her phone.

"Why?" he ask suspiciously.

"I'm supposed to send some pictures to Andre so he can decide if he is happy with the look of 'Werewolf 1'. You're the pattern for the rest of the bunch, and I need to repeat the process tomorrow."

Travis climbed out of the makeup chair. He straightened to his full six feet to tower over the much shorter makeup artist. "Why aren't you working background, like us?"

"Because the pay is better as a makeup artist, and I don't like to run around growling and acting like a monster." Paige aimed her camera at Travis. "Look menacing."

Travis hunched his shoulders. He lifted his furry hands, curled them to make sure the talons were visible, and snarled.

"Perfect." Paige snapped several photos. "I'm glad we can use your own teeth though," she said.

Travis gave her a toothy grin as he stood tall again. His incisors had the look of fangs. The crew would think they were fake, but in reality, lethal.

He was a touch gangly, but the heavy leather jacket Travis had put on added to the width of his shoulders.

Paige texted the photos to her director. "There, let's hope he's happy with this look, I still have five more actors to do."

The trailer door opened. "Hey Paige, here are the rest of the silicone brow ridges." Karl Mullen, the set gopher, carried in a cardboard box with sectioned squares. Inside each cube were several pieces of black silicone, some with tufts of hair glued on.

"Thanks, can you put them on the table over here, please?"

Karl paused to stare at Travis. "Wow." His pale blue eyes opened wide.

Travis lifted his lip in a snarl.

A smile spread across Karl's pink flushed face. "Cool." He continued to stare as he crab-walked to the grey plastic folding table beside Paige's work area. Still staring, he bumped into the table, upsetting bottles of solvents, lotions, paints and cups filled with brushes

"Karl." Paige sighed, and grabbed two rolling bottles before they hit the trailer floor.

"Sorry." He carefully placed his burden in an open spot and flipped a strand of straight brown hair behind one ear.

"My forehead is itching" Travis complained.

"Do not scratch." Paige glanced over her shoulder at the teen, but he was standing idly behind her, leaning on the back of her makeup chair. Not messing up two hours of work.

"Thanks, Karl." Paige said to get the young man moving again.

"No problem." Karl said and exited the trailer, closing the door on the beginnings of a clear autumn day.

Paige returned to refreshing the colours on the pallet from tubes lined up on the workbench. This time she added a brighter green and a darker shade of brown. She wanted to make each werewolf slightly different. The green reminded her of eyeshadow she'd used as a teenager to bring out the colour in her own green eyes. She shuddered at the memory and added a drop of black to darken the makeup.

Her phone pinged and she looked at the return text. It was merely a 'thumbs-up' from the director. Good enough.

She turned to the Travis. "Okay, you're done. Head over to lighting, and see Calvin."

"Will do."

"A word of advice?"

Travis paused by the trailer door and lifted bushy eyebrows at her.

"Don't whinge about what you think about anything, to anyone. Complaining will not get you hired back for another production." Her tone contained a touch of authority. At twenty-nine, Paige out ranked Travis in the pack hierarchy. She also had five years in the film business, and knew how things generally went.

The young man slowly nodded. "Thanks."

Paige gave Travis a smile. "Tell Mindy to come in, please."

***

It was just after nine o'clock in the evening when Paige locked up the makeup trailer. It was good to get out of the close quarters of the small space.

Creating new characters always took time. She was tired, but satisfied with the work she'd done today. Andre was happy with her werewolf designs and that was the most important thing. Once she realized she had to make caricatures out of her subjects, the work had gone quicker. Hopefully, he'd ask her back on his next project.

The outdoor shoots had to be done while the weather held fair and routine to shoot scenes out of sequence. She'd gotten a chance earlier to watch her six subjects act like werewolves.

Paige watched the cast rehearse a chase scene which included the human stars, the evil sorcerer, and his werewolf henchmen. Her werewolves repeatedly ran after Abby and Dan–the heroine and hero–through the woods. Between filming sequences she retouched the werewolf' makeup as needed.

At first, the chase scene contained a comical element. But as the shadows lengthened, with afternoon turning into dusk, a dark edginess emerged in the heroes screams and the werewolf snarls.

By seven o'clock, Andre was satisfied with the results of the shoot and called it good for the day.

After that, Paige rounded up her wolves and taught them how to clean off their makeup. She collected the silicon parts and made sure everyone had the cases for their red contact lenses. "Be back here tomorrow at six in the morning. Whoever's here first, gets into the chair first." Then the kids were gone, leaving her with clean-up and prep for the next day.

A blessed quiet settled around the trailer village as the evening unfolded. Paige breathed in cooler night air and rolled her shoulders to relieve the tightness in her muscles as she walked.

Her actors were all over six feet tall, even the two females. They were specifically chosen to play the band of werewolves by their size. Unfortunately, even with her chair on its lowest setting there was still a lot of stretching and leaning. She was glad Patty, head of makeup, was in charge of the stars. There would be a couple more actors added to Paige's work load in the days to come, but she was good with that.

Paige's running shoes crunched through the dry leaves lining the dirt path to the parking lot. The route wound through various clusters of trailers and sets. Eventually, the trail would bring her to her car in the lot, now mostly empty.

She could hear two male voices in the distance, but recognized them. Abruptly the sound of a diesel generator cut through the quiet as it hammered away. Then several flood lights snapped on in sequence.

Her pace slowed as she passed the portion of the set which was under construction. This was where she went looking for her brother, Reid. His company had been employed to build the fake farmhouse. The build looked close to completion. Once done, the art department would make the building look wind-weathered and abandoned. Every horror movie needed a spooky, haunted house.

Currently there was no one around and she couldn't pick up Reid's scent. He must have left for the day too. It was just as well Paige had driven her own car, she'd told him her hours were unpredictable.

The Cowichan Valley was perfect for the low budget horror movie. The old corn field had been taken over by WingDing Productions almost a month ago. The location was ringed by mountains and forest on three sides. On the fourth, a sliver of ocean could be seen.

The story began as an idyllic romantic picnic for a young couple. The opening scene set under the huge oak tree on the edge of the forest. The script described how the outing turns dark and foreboding when the couple hears chanting in the woods. They decide to leave, but must drive through the scary forest to get back to the main road. Half-way into the wood, their car breaks down and they stumble across some nefarious doings with a sorcerer and werewolves. The couple must flee.

The sorcerer orders his werewolves to catch the girl. She will be his sacrifice in the diabolical plan to bring a demon up from Hell. The sorcerer apparently needed a demon to expand his werewolf army as part of his world domination scheme. Of course in exchange for human souls. Luckily, in the third act the plot is foiled by the young heroes.

Paige had read the script through and found the story as predictable as expected. But the trope was popular with audiences, as long as there was plenty of action, good special effects, and a happy ending with a twist.

She strolled out of the last pool of light, skirting the woods. The path wound past a copse of three hundred year-old-cedar and Garry oak trees, before the artificial security lighting continued again.

Paige knew why Andre had chosen this location. The trees screamed haunted forest. The twisted trunks and erratic shape of the branches, draped in Spanish moss and old man's beard, caught one's imagination. Like now, as the wind picked up and the circle of trees was filled with an inky blackness.

Heighten shapeshifter senses sent her the warning. Something or someone had their eyes on her. Paige eased her brown leather messenger bag across her shoulders to ride her right hip. This left her hands free. Slowly she turned toward the clearing encircled by cedar, arbutus, and oak trees.

"Oscar, is that you?" Paige called out. She guessed it might be the security guard.

Then the light breeze brought a familiar scent to her nose and she relaxed her posture.

"No, I am not Oscar." The reply drifted from among the trees.

A spark of soft blue flame sprang to life. It was no bigger than the end of Paige's pinky, but shed enough light to reveal a female silhouette moving with swift strides across the clearing. The spark obediently trailed behind.

"Hello, Miss Agnes." Paige said when the tall, willowy older female stopped four feet in front of her.

Paige glanced at the blue light, not sure it was a good idea to use power like that. The display might draw attention, but said nothing.

Instead, she swallowed her nervousness and lifted her chin. Seeing the witch from a distance was not nearly as disconcerting as actually speaking to her.

The older woman pursed her lips, like she'd read Paige's thoughts, and the spark went out. Even in the dim light Paige could make out the woman's scowl. Her expression, combined with long grey hair bound in a tight bun, ramrod-straight posture, long black dress, and sensible shoes, made her look the part. Miss Agnes was the local witch. For real.

"Paige St. Claire." Agnes Esme gave her a nod. "What exactly is going on here?" The witch's tone demanded an immediate answer.

"We're filming a movie," Paige said simply. Her fingers curled around the leather strap of her purse. She would not wipe her palms on her jeans in the presence of the witch. It was never good to show weakness.

The old woman folded her hands across her middle and continued to scowl, but said nothing, waiting.

"It's ah...monster movie. Some of the pack is working on the project. It's good employment for the younger members." Paige's words tumbled out in a rush.

"And you."

"Yes, and me, and Reid."

Miss Agnes sniffed disdainfully and turned to glare in the direction of the wood. She raised her left arm and stabbed a bony index finger at the dark clearing at the edge of the trees. "What do you know about that?"

"I don't know–"

"With me," the witch snapped. She abruptly strode away, back the way she'd come, expecting Paige to follow.

Paige inhaled deeply. It was never a good idea to get involved with Miss Agnes, she'd heard the stories. However, if the witch singled you out, it was best to comply. Resigned, Paige exhaled and followed.

The scent of charred grass reached her nose, making it twitch a the acidic smell.

"Look down," Miss Agnes ordered, again she pointed, but this time at their feet. "What do you see?"

"Um, burnt grass." The tiny hairs on her arms lifted, there was more, Paige could feel it.

"Is that all?"

"I can't quite put my finger on it, but there's something not right here." She glanced up into Miss Agnes' steely gaze.

She spread her hands. "Look wider," the witch instructed.

Paige ran her eyes over the scrolls and swirls of the design her night sight revealed spread out on the ground. "There's a pattern. Someone burned the grass into a bunch of glyphs. A circle."

Miss Agnes slowly nodded. "A summoning circle," she said sourly.

"Ah, okay," Paige said, a bit relieved. "This has to do with the film's plot." Paige turned back to the witch. "The bad guy is a sorcerer and needs to gather power so he performs a human sacrifice to raise the demon. In the end he's foiled by 'those pesky kids.'" She gestured with quote hooks. "I forget how they do it, but the heroes beat the sorcerer and save the day. Well, after subduing six werewolves and a demon."

The witch glared at her. "That is patently ludicrous. How could a human best one shapeshifter, let alone six. Or a sorcerer, or a demon? Who would believe such rubbish?"

Paige lifted her hands in a placating gesture. "Hey, it's just a story."

The witch waved Paige's words away. "Regardless, this circle has been drawn correctly," Miss Agnes said.

"Okay," Paige said uncertainly. She glanced down at the design. The shapes almost looked like words spelled out on the ground.

The witch sighed in frustration. "You don't understand. Whoever burned in these glyphs, knew exactly what they were doing. Dark power has been infused into the design. One could actually summon something nasty from the Other Side."

Paige laughed. "You can't be serious."

Without moving a single finger, Miss Agnes ignited the twenty-foot wide clearing in bright yellow light. The dramatic display revealed the details of the sooty, meticulous design in all its sinister glory. Paige was shocked by the sheer size and scale of the work involved. Upon seeing it, a wave of dread swept over her.

"I'm as serious as an executioner's axe."

***

Paige paced the dry ground by her car, her phone at her ear. Her feet stirred up small clouds of dust and particle of dried plants. Shapeshifters didn't get sick. Still, dust allergies outdoors make one's nose itch.

"Valley Island Farm Group."

She rubbed the tip of her nose with the palm of her left hand. "Hi, this is Paige St. Claire, can I speak to Jess Trennor, please?" It had been some time since she'd spoken to the pack mage.

Her car was only one of a handful of vehicles left in the field. She opened the driver's side door and tossed her bag on the passenger seat.

"What is your call pertaining to?"

Was this guy giving her the run around? "Miss Agnes Esme asked me to call."

"One moment, please," he replied crisply.

Her lips twisted as the line clicked and the call was transferred. Apparently the witch's name held some weight. Or maybe dread.

"Jess Trennor," said a composed voice.

"Hello," she swallowed her nervousness. Paige had spent the past five years in Vancouver to avoid the VIC senior members and their deadly pack politics. She felt odd speaking to the pack mage. She hadn't known Jessica very well even before she'd taken on the position. "It's Paige St. Claire, Reid's sister."

"Hi Paige, what can I do for you?"

"I just spoke with Miss Agnes, and we have a situation here."

"Tell me what's going on."

Paige slid into the driver's seat and closed the door. It was unlikely anyone would overhear her words, but there was no point in taking chances. "I'm working on the film set over at the Garry Oaks Preserve, about five minutes Miss Agnes's house. The witch was just here and she says we have an occult circle burned into a clearing. A real one."

"Is the circle set among a ring of trees?"

"Yes, it is. I wouldn't have bothered you with this except Miss Agnes is very concerned. She said the glyphs have been 'drawn properly.'" Paige mimicked the witches tone."She thinks the circle could actually be used to summon something. I'm guessing this is bad."

There was silence on the other end. Paige merely waited as she heard the mage take a breath.

"Did you take any photos?"

"I did, tell me where to send them."

Less than a minute later the mage received the circle photos. Again Paige waited on the line for her reaction.

"You were right to call." Paige could hear the tension in the mage's voice. This was bad.

From the background noise, other people were in the room with Jess. Someone made the grave comment, "There was no circle last time."

"There was, but it was more primitive. The creature used the trees as the circle, that's why they were burnt," the mage responded. "We figured that out later, after we sent it back."

"The oaks are an anchor point, this could be an issue." Someone else commented.

"True," Jess said.

What was an anchor point? What happened last time? Paige wanted to ask, but knew better. If Jess wanted to share the information she would, but the feeling of unease in Paige's gut was growing.

"Paige?"

"I'm here."

"The circle's design might be a coincidence, but bears investigating. Can you look into this for us? I'd do it, but I have a few pressing things on my plate right now. You must have heard about Courtney?"

"Yes, Reid said she was under arrest for attempted murder."

"She is. We also have a situation in Arizona which has Lottie, and other resources tied up. So we're a bit shorthanded at the moment." Lottie Fistbinder was head of security, Paige new that too. Reid had brought her up-to-date on the pack's changes.

"Sure, no problem." The words just popped out, and immediately Paige knew she would regret them.

"Good. Find out who created the design and where they got the idea. Call me, when you know something. I'll need you to cancel the circle too. Just in case." Jess gave Paige a set of instructions to follow to do just that. "You should have no problem, if this is a real summoning circle, you'll feel it when the power is neutralized."

"Okay." Paige said tentatively.

"And Paige?"

"Yes?"

"Delete those photos from your phone, they're dangerous." The call ended.

No task became more pleasant with the waiting. Paige left her car and retraced her steps to the copse of trees. The same sensation of dread crept over her. On her first encounter, the feeling had been negligible. Now there was a presence, something waiting, and the feeling was becoming more tangible. As her apprehension grew stronger, her wolf wanted out. She clamped down hard on the instinct to change shape. That wouldn't help the situation.

Jaw clenched, Paige walked the circumference of the shape. As Jess instructed, she found the most northerly point of the shape. Then headed to the far side of the circle, well away from the well-trod path.

She was careful not to step on any of the three-inch-wide lines of blackened grass.

Paige stopped under a twisted, sky-reaching Garry oak. The charred smell was thicker, and coated the back of her throat.

Jess' instructions ran through her mind. The tasks were simple enough, but she'd never attempted anything like this before. She'd only ever used her magic to change shape. This, this something beyond her experience.

Paige closed her eyes and mentally reached inside her. She ran virtual fingertips across the reservoir of magic she possessed. Like every other shapeshifter, the indigo pool of magic waited next to her soul. The power was dormant until she used her will to tap it.

She visualized dipping her fingers below the surface. Instantaneously, the power engulfed her. With sheer force of will, Paige held back on the change. She forced down the urge to become her wolf.

Instead, she opened her eyes and placed her running shoe a foot into the circle and dragged her heel, traversing the lines. "*Intermissum*," she breathed the word out slowly at the same time. The magic moved through her and flow into the Latin word. Like a stone tossed into a pond, ripples spread out to engulf the circle, tightening around it. She felt a fracture, like a window breaking. The glass falling in a tinkling shower. Then there was silence and the feeling of dread was gone.

The circle was broken.

***

It was mid-morning the next day, and a gentle misty rain fell on set. Paige walked over to the long trailer which held the props and art departments.

Paige found Shirley Grayson, a tall, freckled black woman who was the head of the art department. Her long dark hair was caught up in a gold scarf. The colour was close to that of the paint she was spraying on a long-handled knife hung from a rafter by a wire. The blade was covered in blue masking tape with only the handle exposed. She turned her head to see who entered.

The mask Shirley was wearing made Paige realize she shouldn't have opened the door without knocking. "Sorry," she said, and began to back out, closing the door.

"No worries." Shirley straightened and removed the mask. "Leave the door open, let the fresh air in. I'm done painting for the moment."

Paige nodded and flipped the bungee cord over the door handle to keep the portal open. "How's it going?" She nodded at the knife. The blade appeared realistic and deadly, even though she knew this couldn't be the case. Shirley had painted golden symbols on the handle.

"Good, I'm ahead of schedule for once." Shirley used the crook of her elbow to wipe the perspiration from her face. "Did you need something?"

"I just had a question."

"Shoot."

"Your guys made the summoning circle, right?"

"Yeah, Marvin did. It turned out well I thought."

"Very realistic," Paige said. "I just wondered where you got the design."

Shirley lifted one dark eyebrow at Paige. "Why?"

"I was thinking of using the circle design in scene forty-seven, one of the werewolves has his shirt torn off."

Shirley nodded. "For the beef-cake shot?"

"Yes, and he's supposed to have a tattoo. I thought it would be cool to repeat the design."

"Good idea." Shirley crossed the floor to a grey plastic table setup under a window and Paige followed. "We got it from this old book." She grabbed a threadbare, hardcover book about a foot long. The dull grey cover was worn so bad there were no words left on the front cover or spine. One bright orange sticky note protruded from between the pages. Shirley flipped the raw-edge parchment open to the bookmarked page. In stunning detail the circle from the clearing was exposed across both pages, the full width of the book.

"Where did you get this?" Paige accepted the weight of the tomb in her hands. Immediately, a surge of dread shot up her spine. She almost dropped the book. To cover her shock, Paige gripped the tome with both hands and forced herself to ignore the unpleasant feeling emanating from the book.

"I don't know. Marvin came in with it. It was his idea."

Paige swallowed hard and pasted on a smile. "Can I borrow this? I'll speak to Marvin and let him know I have it."

"Sure," the other woman said distractedly and picked up her paint gun. "Leave the door open, please."

Paige left the trailer. The rain was coming down harder. She flipped up the hood on her green rain jacket.

Water droplets were making a wet pattern on the cover of the old book. Still, Paige couldn't bring herself to put the volume under her coat. The book smelt faintly of rotten eggs and something metallic she couldn't identify. She pulled her coat sleeves over her hands one at a time, so her skin won't have to touch the cover material. It looked like calf skin, but something told her it wasn't.

The bulk of the crew who were not required for filming had scattered. Probably to avoid the rain. A red-coated male jogged by Paige, he snagged her attention. It was Marvin, heading down the path.

He might be going to the parking lot, but somehow Paige doubted it and decided to follow. She regretted not dumping the book in her trailer first. The longer she held the thing, the more uncomfortable it made her.

Paige quickly caught up with the husky male. The rain plastered his dark hair to his head and his light jacket was soaked through. He stood hands on hips studying the burnt circle.

"Son of a gun," Marvin said.

"Is it ruined?" Paige asked. For a brief moment she hoped the rain might have destroyed the arcane shape completely, but no, the circle looked intact. At least there was no odd feelings around the location anymore.

He glanced down at her. "It looks okay. I hope we can get the scene shot before it's damaged. We weren't supposed to have any rain for days yet."

Paige slid her eyes over to the opposite side, where she'd broken the dark magic. "So what happens now?" She could see where the lines were breached, but apparently Marvin couldn't.

"We'll have to wait to see how it is after the rain. If there is damage we can repair it with paint." His eyes dropped to her hands. "Why do you have Karl's book?"

***

"There's a full moon tonight," Karl said. "The rains have all but stopped."

"We could shoot the summoning scene, and then send the video to the computer graphics team. It takes longer to create the effects than it does to edit an entire film." Andre remarked, arms folded over his chest as he stood in his trailer studying the story board. His curly blond hair cascaded down his shoulders and shifted like a short cape when he moved his head. "We need this shoot to go perfect. I need to stay on schedule." He glanced at his wrist watch. "It's five o'clock now. I think we can fit this shoot in today." He turned to Karl. "Find Denice for me, let her know scene one-forty is a go."

Karl smiled, his flat blue gaze locked on a drawing. It depicted a demon rising from the centre of the circle. On the ground, inside the shape, was sketched the bound figure of the female star.

It wouldn't be long now until his master was free. "Right away, Andre."

***

Paige managed to bluff Marvin into thinking she was looking for Karl. Okay, lied. Geez, what kind of person was she turning into? She stalked to her car and drove to a two-story white clapboard house half a kilometre from the set.

Miss Agnes was standing on the veranda, like she had been waiting for Paige to arrive.

"Here, please take it!" Paige thrust the nasty book at the old woman. "Jess said you'd know what to do with it."

The witch plucked the hardcover from Paige's hands. "Of course I do." She used two fingers and turned to drop the book into what looked to Paige like a coal bucket. Who still used coal?

The book flopped open to the circle diagram, all on its own. Paige took a step back.

"We need you to go back and find every picture, drawing, or photograph of the circle and destroy them."

"What? Why?"

"Because they can be used to either redraw the circle or, used itself, as a summoning circle." Agnes explained patiently. "While you're gone, I'll deal with this." She looked into the metal bucket with revulsion. "I think a visit to the blacksmith is in order."

When Paige got back to the set, Travis and the other shapeshifter, Mindy, were hanging out by her trailer door.

"Paige, Jess called us." He gave her a meaningful look.

"Oh?"

"We're to follow your lead." Mindy came to stand beside Travis and gravely gave Paige a nod.

"Okay," she said uncertainly.

"Paige!"

A shout came from behind her. She turned to identify who was trying to get her attention. It was Marvin.

He jogged over and frowned down at her. "Where's your radio? I've been looking for you for the past ten minutes. We've got Tony glued up, we need you to finish his makeup. We can't bring him here, his tail is too bulky."

"Sorry, I left my stuff inside. I'll be right there, let me grab my case."

Marvin glanced at Travis and Mindy.

"We had a makeup malfunction, but it's all fixed now." Mindy smiled at Marvin, as sweetly as three inch fangs would allow.

Eyebrows raised he turned and strode away.

Paige turned back to the shapeshifters. "I need you two to find all the circle diagrams and destroy them."

"Like Andre's story board?" Travis looked around them to ensure they spoke privately.

"Yes."

"How?" Mindy asked.

"Burn them. They look like this." She showed them the photos on her phone. "I've dealt with the actual circle already."

A slow smile spread across his face. "We're on it," Travis said.

The shape shifters jogged off.

Paige collected her case along with the radio she should have clipped to her belt. At the props/art trailer she swung open the big door and was greeted by a nightmare.

Tony was not only six and a half feet tall, he was broad and well-muscled. His torso, arms, neck, and face were painted deep indigo-blue. Ram-shaped horns spiralled out from each side of his head. The pale bone matched the hooves on his feet. Out of the back of his blue jeans, the demon sported a long blue tail which lay on the floor behind him. He gave her a finger wave. "Can we do this standing up?" He batted long eyelashes at her.

Paige laughed.

Thirty minutes later, all the principal characters were in position at the clearing. Even though the rain had stopped, heavy black clouds made the atmosphere feel thick with expectation. Thankfully, the area still felt inert to Paige.

Abby and Dan were bound. She lay inside the circle. He was outside, so they could confess their undying love before they foiled the evil plan and escaped.

Andy, the sorcerer, stood ready to invoke the summoning. Tony waited off camera to magically appear in the centre of the glyphs.

"We're missing two werewolves," Andre shouted. "Where are my werewolves?"

Mindy ran forward and took a position at Andy's left side. Travis rushed up and dropped down to kneel at the sorcerer's right. Neither new arrival said anything, but Travis gave Paige a shallow nod. Relief flooded her, she wanted to call Jess, but it would have to wait.

"Looks great, doesn't it?" Karl whispered into Paige's ear, making her jump. How had he snuck up on her?

Karl smirked and walked away, parking himself at Andre's elbow.

"And...mark." Andre projected his voice over the set and all quieted. The clap-board was held up, filmed, and taken away. "Sorcerer." This was Andy's cue to begin.

Andy raised his hands slowly and began to chant. Tension began to build as he spoke some Latin phrases.

To Paige, most of the chant sounded like gibberish to her, still, the words sounded good and scary.

As the scene progressed, she frowned while the chanting continued. No one moved. The heroes should be doing something by now. The actors didn't look like they were following the script. Then she felt it, the gathering air pressure, the feeling of wrongness.

The cast and crew was enthralled.

Paige noticed Andre was chanting along with Andy, but he wasn't repeating the same gibberish as the actor. Oddly, the director and Karl, his assistant, were rocking back and forth while Karl whispered into Andre's ear.

Finally Andy held out his left hand and Travis placed the knife Shirley had created on his palm. Or was it? The blade looked lethal. There was no sun, and yet light glanced of the blade.

A steady hum filled the air, but it wasn't coming from the circle.

"Holy crap," Paige gasped. She grabbed her phone out of her back pocket. It was searing hot to the touch and flipped out of her hands. The device landed in the mud several feet away, between her and Tony. Instantly, the ground dried and cracks radiated out from the phone.

The big blue actor/demon raised one black eyebrow at her. He opened his mouth to comment but was cut off when a cone of bright red light shot up from the phone. The light expanded two-feet wide, stabbing the air.

"He comes!" Karl shouted spreading his arms and walking slowly forward, toward the mobile phone lying in the dirt.

The light created a blazing red door. Heat and the stench of rotten eggs bathed Paige as she stumbled back.

"Oh, no." She'd forgotten to delete the photos.

Transfixed, the crew stared as the door cracked open. White-hot forged heat poured out of the portal and with it, a figure emerged. The demon, who could have been a twin to Tony, except instead of blue, this demon was deep red and not wearing any clothes. His split pupils surveyed the scene, flat and reptilian. He opened his mouth and raised one clawed finger. "Was that my cue?" his smug baritone voice rolled out.

"No, it wasn't." Miss Agnes said, striding past Paige and the rest of the crew. She came to a stop, mere inches away from the demon. "*Intermissum,*" the witch spat and brought a blacksmith's hammer down on the phone. The case shattered in a shower of glass and plastic, breaking the circle.

In a blink, the demon was gone.

The witch's gaze locked on to Karl. "Sub-demon Mullen, corrupter of souls, we cast you out."

"Travis, Mindy, take Karl," Paige ordered. Now was not the time to worry about staying hidden. Maybe now was the time for people to know about shapeshifters. They'd just seen a demon.

Travis and Mindy shifted. Gasps and fearful exclamations rippled through the people as the crew fell back. Gone were the faux werewolves. In their place, shapeshifter nightmares in half-form. Huge, fanged, and fierce.

Karl scuttled back in a panic. As soon as he was no longer touching Andre, the director had collapsed to the ground.

Just as Karl turned to run, Mindy plucked him from the ground. He fought, clawing at her arm. Mindy gave him a shake and his human glamour slid off to reveal an ugly, twisted red and charcoal creature.

"Travis," Miss Agnes said. "Use the knife."

He grabbed the gold-handled weapon from Andy and looked to Paige.

"Stab the sub-demon, the steel will send it back to the Other Side." The witch came forward, still grasping the hammer. Her posture said if he didn't do it, she would. Mindy had to use both fists to hold the demon. She needed help.

Paige pushed past the witch. "This is my fault, I'll do it."

Travis tossed Paige the blade.

"Nooooo. Don't want to go back!" The creature struggled as Travis grabbed sinewy limbs.

Miss Agnes looked steadily down at Paige. "Do it."

In her hand, Paige knew the dagger was a prop, it was useless to stab. Instead, Paige dragged the tip of the dagger down the sub-demons forearm. It squealed in pain as red leathery skin split, revealing an angry heat. In an explosion of ashes, the lessor demon was gone.

The four coughed and wiped at the grey cinders coating them. More ash floated to the ground.

"I never liked Karl," someone in the crew said.

Paige wiped ashes out of one eye. "I stand corrected, guys. Your half-forms are pretty scary." Travis and Mindy laughed, exposing long fangs.

Patty helped Andre too his feet. He looked around dazed and then his glare locked onto a cameraman. "Tell me you got that."

Miss Agnes folded her hands over her middle. "Cut," she said with a satisfied nod.

The Shape of Us

H

ow are you feeling?" I asked the young boy lying on the hospital gurney. He was pale as the sheet that covered him. When he turned his head to look at me I saw gold roll over his irises. Anyone else would have missed it, but I am trained to look for the tell-tale signs that hinted at a shapeshifter about to lose control.

He didn't answer me and his eyes were unfocused. Not good.

"You're going to be okay Dylan." I said in a steady voice. I infused my tone with a touch of influence and he started to breathe easier.

I put my hand on his shoulder and with my fingers, I brushed dark hair aside to touch the back of his neck. I made a physical connection between us and he finally focused on me. "Do you know me?" I asked as I watched the gold flecks in his eyes recede slightly. "Do you know who I am?"

"Yeah, "he croaked with a flash of relief in his expression.

The familiar scent of male child shapeshifter was overlaid with fear and something else I couldn't identify.

Being this close to one of my pack members resurrected the sadness I kept suppressed most of the time. I was still a part of them, I reminded myself. I just wasn't required to be involved in the day to day affairs of the pack, according to our alpha.

"You're Jess; you used to teach us kids meditation stuff." He was responsive now, that was a good sign. It meant he was regaining his control.

"Yes I am and yes I did." I smiled at him and pushed away my loneliness. I had other priorities at the moment.

I concentrated and pulled a thread of surface energy into me. I buffered it. Gently, sending calming messages with my touch, to his nervous system. A casual observer wouldn't't have noticed anything, other than Dylan's shoulders inching down from his ears.

"Do you remember your breathing techniques? What should you do first?" I asked.

"Take slow, deep breaths." Dylan answered with his eyes locked on mine. "Count backwards from fifty to one."

"Excellent, give me three good ones to start." Dylan slowly took a long shaky breath.

I turned to the man seated just outside the examination cubical. This was the person who had ridden in the ambulance with Dylan. I picked up the chart and walked over to him.

"Hi, I'm Jessica Raiway." I don't usually give out my last name, but right now I needed to inspire trust. "I'm an RN here at Fortunate Saint, and a former Farm kid myself. I know Dylan's mom." I offered him my hand.

"John Foggle, I'm Dylan's science teacher." The thin wiry man who looked to be in his late forties stood and took my hand. His handshake was soft and his palm damp. "Pleased to meet you," he said as watery blue eyes behind wire frame glasses, darted around the ER.

The teacher smelled of sweat and unease. His forehead was damp which made his comb-over stick to his head. With his hunched shoulders, I got the feeling he wanted to bolt.

"Can you tell me what happened?" I raised the clipboard and clicked my pen open to document the incident.

"No, sorry." Foggle shook his head vigorously and shrugged. "I didn't see what happened." He pushed wispy strands of hair out of his eyes. "I was alerted when Dylan's lab partner shouted that Dylan was unconscious and had fallen onto the floor."

"Do you know if Dylan's lab partner noticed any symptoms Mr. Foggle?" I watched his eyes, or tried to, he kept glancing away.

"That was the first thing I asked Eddy, he didn't know what happened either." Mr. Foggle shrugged again.

"Eddy who?"

"Ah, Eddy Rippley."

"Okay, thanks." I could get rid of this guy then. "I'll stay with Dylan until his mom gets here." I tucked my pen into my scrub pocket and tucked the clipboard under my arm. "I'm sure you have to get back to the school, I know it's in the middle of the work day for you."

I couldn't talk to Dylan until this guy was gone. I needed to know what had happened and the type of questions I was going to ask were not for civilian ears.

"I suppose that would be okay, since Dylan knows you and you work here." He looked at my Fortunate Saint General Hospital ID clipped to my lilac scrubs to reassure himself that everything I told him was in line.

I did my best to look trustworthy.

I turned back to Dylan. "I called the Farm, and Lottie said your mom was on her way. She left right after the school called her. She should be here shortly, if I know her at all." Dylan nodded as he inhaled and exhaled slowly.

"All right Dylan," Mr. Foggle said. He stood and patted the bed rail making it rattle. "I'll have the school call your mother tomorrow to see how you are and when we can expect you back in class."

Dylan nodded again, but kept his focus on me and let out his fifth long slow breath. Smart. He knew he had to completely regain control of himself despite the strange place and scents.

For shapeshifters, control is everything. It must be maintained at all times if we are to live alongside standard humans.

"Take care of yourself Dylan." Foggle nodded at me then headed toward the sliding doors.

I waited for the teacher to be out of ear shot before I pulled the screening curtains partly closed. "Can you tell me what happened?" I grasped his wrist and glanced at my watch to clock his pulse.

His pale skin felt grainy under my fingers. I leaned closer and breathed in his scent, he smelled like black licorice. Weird.

"I don't know, we were doing blood type identification, you know when you stick your finger and put a drop of blood on a slide? To figure out if you are A or B positive or negative or maybe O?" He let out a long breath as he spoke.

"Yes I remember how it goes." I put his wrist down and covered him with the sheet. I made a note on the chart. "Then what happened?" I pulled my stethoscope out of my pocket.

"I was done looking at the slides and was drinking my juice waiting for Eddy to finish. I got dizzy and fell off my stool. I think I hit my head on the counter because I passed out. I woke up in the ambulance."

I frowned and examined his scalp for contusions.

Nothing. "Can you lift your chin for me?" Again, nothing, he hadn't been clipped on the jaw either.

Although Dylan would have healed quickly like all shapeshifters, there would still have been a bruise.

"Where did you stick your finger?" I asked.

"Right here," Dylan said, showing me the index finger on his left hand.

I could still see the puncture which was odd. His shifter metabolism should have healed the wound completely by now. "How long ago did you puncture your finger to get the blood sample?"

"First period, I think probably around nine-thirty." He lay back against the pillows like he was exhausted.

It was almost eleven o'clock now. Whatever that was wrong with him was also affecting Dylan's rate of healing. I took the rest of Dylan's vital signs and wrote them down on his chart.

Shapeshifters rarely fainted. We have immune systems that block out viruses and disease, we heal quickly from broken bones, and while we are not impervious to injury, we are exceedingly hard to injure or kill.

"Do you know what's wrong with me?" His blue eyes met mine and there were still gold flecks in their depths. "Am I gonna die like my Dad?"

He swallowed nervously and I handed him a cup of water. I added a straw for him to wet his throat. Dylan's skin was pale. He felt wrong, smelt wrong and I didn't know why. Even so, I had to reassure him he would be all right.

"I don't think you're going to die." I gave him a level look as I slid my stethoscope back into my shirt pocket. "We'll have to run some tests to find out why you passed out. Have you had anything else happen lately that could explain this episode?"

"Like what?" The boy wrinkled his brow and a thatch of wavy black hair fell over his forehead.

"Have you hit your head, have you had any sickness or eaten something you shouldn't?" I suggested.

"No. And I don't get sick, none of us do." Then he said quietly "Except my Dad."

I let that last remark go by without comment; it wasn't up to me to explain Julian's death. That was his mother's job.

"Have you had any trouble shifting? When was the last time you shifted?" I needed to know, but this information was not going into the hospital records.

He shook his head. "I shifted after supper last night. Me and Eddy went hunting squirrels for a while before chores."

"Is this the same Eddy that's your lab partner?" I placed my hand over his sternum. I felt the pulse of his shapeshifter magic. It was regular and strong.

"Yeah, Eddy Rippley. He lives down the road from the Farm."

"I know the Rippley family." I nodded. "They're all red foxes."

"Yeah. Well, we met half way up the road on the new land." I was encouraged that some colour was coming back into his cheeks as he spoke.

"Catch any squirrels?"

"Nah," Dylan sighed. "But Ben said to keep practicing."

"Yes, Ben believes in practice makes perfect. He told me the same thing when I was a kid." Not so much about squirrels, not that I wanted to hunt a squirrel let alone catch one. "Where's this new land you went hunting on?"

"It's off Herd Road beside the Rippley's place, down from the Farm going into town. We were checking it out and these black squirrels were running all over the place so we chased them." And marking the territory no doubt, I bit back a smile and kept that thought to myself.

"I wish I'd have caught one, I would have taken it to my mom." Dylan said with regret.

"I'll bet she would've been pleased if you had. Did you find anything else besides squirrels?" His eyes met mine at the question. Their colour had settled down to a mundane blue.

"No, just animal spoor, there are lots of deer there. That will be good in the fall for hunting."

"What's your animal?" I was pretty sure Dylan was a wolf. Even though his scent was off, I could detect the underlining trace of wolf.

"I'm a wolf like my mom and dad," he whispered with a hint of fear in his tone.

"Wolves are strong and nobody is stronger than your mom, that's why she's our Alpha." That got a pleased smile out of Dylan.

I noticed he now had moisture on his forehead and upper lip. His system was burning through something. I noted this symptom on the chart.

"Drink more water, it seems to be helping," I said and handed Dylan the refilled cup. Hydration was always a good thing and it gave Dylan a modicum of control back which would help calm him further.

I wondered where the doctor was, he should have been here by now. I called his service right after I had called the Farm to ensure the Alpha was notified.

Speak of the devil, the curtain slid further open, and the six foot, greying grandfatherly figure of Doctor Charles Hector stepped into the examining area.

He put his hands on his hips and leaned back on his heels. He assessed Dylan with friendly brown eyes. His basketball sized belly stretched his worn blue shirt which caused it to hang billowy and loose over his tan trousers. "Well young man, what have you done to yourself?"

Dylan's eyes went round and he glanced at me like he was in trouble. "It's okay Dylan," I said, patting his foot under the sheet.

Charles Hector had been the Vancouver Island Clan's doctor for as long as I could remember. Doctor Hector had been treating the pack members for every ailment that afflicted us for about three decades.

While it's true we are rarely sick, we do need broken bones set and fish hooks removed among other things. This service gained the invaluable trust and gratitude of the VIC, which is rare for a standard human to achieve.

Rarer still, was that a standard human was allowed to know our secret. Doctor Hector knew he treated shapeshifters and not a whisper of our existence had ever been leaked.

I greeted him and gave report to the doctor while his eyes studied Dylan and his hands went through a cursory examination.

At that moment, Lasha Cooper, Dylan's mother came through the unit doors and made a beeline over to her only child.

Lasha was in her late thirties and about ten years older than me. She was tall and athletic with the same blue eyes and dark hair as her son. Lasha was the Alpha of the Vancouver Island Clan or VIC and had been for the past five years. This last year on her own since her mate and husband Julian Cooper, had passed away.

"Dylan!" Lasha's voice was higher than normal with stress but no gold rolled over her eyes I noted. "What happened?" She put her hands on either side of her boy's face and searched him for answers.

"We're trying to determine just that, Lasha," Doctor Hector said.

Dylan bore this examination for a couple of moments before sighing, "Mom." He dragged out the word painfully.

Lasha reluctantly let him go.

"Doctor Hector, thank you for coming." Lasha smiled at the older man.

"No problem. I got the call from my service and knew I should be here for you and Dylan." He gave her a warm smile and his composed demeanor help calm Lasha down.

Then he turned to me. "Jessica, can you please see if we can get Dylan in for an MRI scan today?"

"Will do," I said.

"Now let's have a listen to your respiratory system Dylan."

While Hector was examining Dylan, I went back to the desk to see if there was an opening in the schedule for him.

In human shape, our bodies look exactly like standard humans. The only difference is the magic we carry that allows us to shift, which is undetectable. It also keeps us in excellent health and extends our lifespan past the standard human range. The existence of shifter magic is never disclosed to anyone, not even trusted pack allies like Doctor Hector. We swear an oath to keep it so.

I returned to the cubical with positive news and an orderly followed me back to take Dylan downstairs for the scan.

"The lab will send a tech over to get his blood as well; I'll follow up on that." I said to Hector and Lasha.

"Thank you Jessica, you are on top of things as always." The doctor beamed at me and I couldn't help feeling pleased with his approval. I'd known Doctor Hector as my GP and then my working associate for a long time. His praise was like being told by your grandpa you did good.

"You're in good hands Dylan." I leaned closer to tuck in the sheet around him. "Remember to breathe." I whispered as our eyes met and he nodded.

Lasha kissed her boy's forehead and allowed the orderly to take him away. Doctor Hector followed.

"Jess, I'm so glad you were here." Lasha smiled stiffly at me but it didn't reach her ice blue eyes.

I ignored the frost. "I am too. Dylan was about two seconds away from shifting, he was that scared."

Her fake smile slid away.

"Oh God," she whispered. A shaking hand covering her mouth.

"Exactly," I said. "Someone should have called me as soon as you knew he was going to the ER. This could have gone a whole other way without me here to keep him calm."

We both knew the devastation a shapeshifter could cause; especially with a shifter as young and inexperienced as Dylan.

"He hasn't been practicing his meditation has he?" I drilled her with my gaze. She may be the VIC Alpha, but I am the VIC Mage. "You know the damage a kid his size can do, even at ten years old he could kill somebody." I kept my voice low, only for her hearing.

"You're right of course, I just, I mean, there has just been so little time lately for anything."

"I knew when I moved out this was going to happen. You promised me you would keep up the classes. I trained Katherine specifically to take over for me." I folded my arms over my chest and tried not to glare at the other woman.

She at least didn't try an alpha stare on me. Alphas are all about power and domination. With every situation they expect the other members to drop their eyes and submit.

That's not part of my job description. As mage, I am expected to ensure the rules and policies are followed, even by the alpha.

"Yes, well, that didn't happen and now the kids are behind and rusty in their techniques. I thought I would have everything under control by now, but I don't." She swallowed and gritted her teeth before looking back at me. "We need you back Jess." Her blue eyes were candid as she looked at me, although the words were still tough for her to say. "I understand that now."

I raised my eyebrows at her in surprise. That had been quite the admission. "What about the way I destabilize your powerbase?" This had been Lasha's argument to get me to move off the Farm. She wanted me to put some space between me and the other councillors. I had to admit she wasn't completely wrong about that. With Julian gone, many had expected Lasha to step down.

I had agreed to move away to prevent a rift from developing, those same VIC members had expected me to tell her to give up the alpha role. Easily said, but who would take over?

We didn't have a female interested in challenging Lasha for the top spot. We also didn't have a couple interested in taking on the joint headache either.

Every unattached male was jockeying to take Julian's place and I was glad not to be witnessing that scrum anymore. The males had to be careful; they couldn't press Lasha too much. She had a year to decide what she wanted to do, or who she would Choose to be at her side.

I frowned as I realized we were coming to the end of that time soon.

With me living off the farm, it simplified matters and gave Lasha the opportunity to show she could run the pack on her own. She didn't need a mate to do that.

I have to confess it was good to be away from the politics, even if it was lonely at times being on my own. And yet as the pack mage, I am something apart from the rest of them anyway, because I can't shift. I have no animal form.

"I've taken steps to remedy the imbalance in power. It should be fine now for you to come back."

I didn't know what she meant, but I didn't want to discuss this right here, right now.

"You seriously want me to move back?"

"Yes," she said, sounding sincere, if stressed.

I needed to think about her offer to return to the pack and to the only family I've ever known.

"Where's your escort?" I just realized she had no one at her back.

"He's parking the car." A single tear tracked down her cheek. I immediately felt guilty, she was worried about Dylan, and I turned the discussion into a political argument.

"I'm sorry, come have a seat." I led the way to the waiting area where Lasha sat down in one of the uncomfortable brown chairs and took a moment to gather her composure.

"Can I get you anything?" I asked.

She just shook her head and wiped her eyes and worked on getting a grip on herself.

"Dylan isn't Julian, Lasha." I sensed I knew why she was upset. I placed a consoling hand on her shoulder for a moment. "He'll be fine, believe me. I'll make sure you can take him home as soon as possible. Today even, if he seems recovered enough and if we get all the tests completed."

Lasha closed her eyes briefly, breathing in and out slowly. When she opened them again I could see the VIC Alpha was firmly back in place.

She looked back at me steadily. "I should have called you as soon as I heard, I'm sorry. I've had a lot on my plate and I'm out of the habit of communicating important information." She looked at me speculatively for a minute and seemed to come to a decision, "We've been having some problems."

I looked at Lasha in shock. One, an Alpha does not apologize and two, what problems could the pack have that they couldn't take care of themselves?

"Please sit down." Lasha gestured to the plastic chair next to her. I dropped into the seat. My uniform did nothing to cushion the hard plastic seat. "You've probably haven't heard yet about the Wild Rose Pack. They're planning on going public. Up until lately no one knew there were any shapeshifters anywhere except in California and you know how badly that has gone."

"Yes, I've seen the news; protests, shootings, basically a disaster. The public is terrified." I brushed my auburn bangs off my forehead in frustration and smoothed the loose strands into my braid.

Lasha nodded, her eyes meeting mine as an equal in the first time in a long time.

"The media is all over the rumours and they're trying to discover if there are other shapeshifter packs in North America." She pushed her own black hair behind her ears and took a calming breath. "Our security has uncovered rumours of shapeshifters here on the Island. We don't know if someone leaked information but the investigation continues."

"So what about Wild Rose?" I asked.

"Lottie has tracked rumours about the Wild Rose Pack's existence. Apparently some blogger has reported sightings of shapeshifters. So I spoke with Mike Sydorenko last week; he's the new Alpha for Wild Rose. He said he wants to go public, but he just hasn't decided when or how he will do it."

"Mike Sydorenko took down Hans Jacobson? Holy crap! Was the Challenge to the death or to first blood?"

"First blood, Hans was tired of it all and ready to give it up. I think he didn't want to deal with the politics and upheaval going public will spawn."

"What did Madge say?" Madge Gracie was the Mage for Wild Rose.

"I haven't spoken to Madge, I was hoping you had."

"No." I shook my head. "I haven't heard a word about this. I'll call her as soon as I'm off today."

"That would be great. I'd like to know what she advises. I discussed the possibility of going public with some of our councillors just to gauge how they felt. According to my unofficial poll, we are not ready to take the 'going public' step. There is so much controversy about our kind and no one in the pack wants to deal with the fallout, let alone the fear and shunning." She looked back at me. "If Wild Rose goes, I hope we can continue to come in under the radar until our members adjust to the idea."

"I know the race issue is scaring everyone." I said. "Once people understand that shapeshifters are just as human as the next person, a lot of this will die down." I said trying to reassure her. "Well, as long as shifters continue to practice discipline and control," I qualified.

"You and I know that, however the council doesn't think the general public will understand and frankly I am not sure we are ready for that radical step. Better yet, I hope Mike reconsiders his position," Lasha said.

"That would be for the best," I agreed.

Lasha looked at the door where Dylan had disappeared. "I don't trust these places, not since I lost Julian here." Lasha said sharply.

We shared a look. Julian's death was suspicious to both of us. He had died in this very hospital over a year ago and we didn't know why.

All we knew was the official cause of death was a burst appendix and internal bleeding. This is unheard of for a shapeshifter, but how could anyone dispute it after Doctor Hector had confirmed it.

There was no way we could explain to the coroner the difference between a standard human and shapeshifter physiology without coming out to the general public. To the coroner, Julian's death could have been prevented if he had received treatment in time, but it still was a normal death.

To us, it was suspect. Shapeshifters don't have organ failure, we regenerate our organs much like a standard human liver can regenerate if damaged. However our systems are much quicker and it is true for all our organs. Sometimes I think we are the next step in evolution, but other times, when we lose control, not so much.

Doctor Hector was just as puzzled over Julian's death as the rest of us. And though he thought there is always an exception to the rule that all shapeshifters are immune to that type of death, I would still feel better if we knew what had actually happened to Julian.

"We're having trouble obtaining the land for the clinic." Lasha sighed.

"Is this the new land Dylan was talking about? He said he was there yesterday."

"Yes, more than likely. I think someone is trying to block our plans for the land. Obtaining the permits and zoning has been a nightmare. Every issue has turned into a road block." Lasha's hands curled into fists. "I can't point to anything definitive but it all smells wrong."

"You're worried someone actually knows about us, more than rumors?" I causally looked around the waiting room as I quietly said it. Nobody was paying us any attention. "If someone suspects—," I started to say then I caught a scent I hadn't experienced in a long, long time.

I instinctively zeroed in on the source and he stood just inside the sliding doors surveying the ER. Iain Trennor was no doubt looking for Lasha.

He was over six foot with dark hair, cut severely short on the sides. The rest of his dark waves had their own way on the crown of his head before falling onto his tanned forehead.

He had a firm square jaw, just this side of stubborn. It was dusted with five o'clock shadow and he had deep green eyes that made you think of the ferns that grew wild all over the island when you looked deeply into them.

I watched his reaction as his thick dark eyebrows gathered in a frown as he too scented the air and then targeted me with those intense green eyes.

Iain Trennor strode toward us like he was aiming for me. The soft T-shirt and faded jeans did nothing to conceal his hard, lean, body and accentuated the power of his well-defined muscles. God he looked good, better than I had ever seen him.

Iain's frown cleared as he got closer. His eyes locked on me and that sexy half smile that I so remembered appeared on his lips.

I experienced a mild panic attack as realized I had been completely blindsided. Lasha should have told me.

I just looked up at him as he came and stood right in front of me.

"Hi." Was all Iain said.

We stared at each other for a moment and I felt his gaze slide over my face and body. It felt as intimate as his touch had once had been.

My breath stuck in my throat, it was constricted with emotion. Seven years and not one word I reminded myself. I had no idea how to process this. I decided not to, at least not where others could see my pain.

"I have to get back to work." I said, as I stood up and tore my eyes off of Iain. I looked over at our alpha. "I'll help you all I can, you know that. I'll also speak with Madge and find out what's going on with Wild Rose."

"Drop by the Farm tomorrow afternoon and we can discuss this more." Lasha stood too. She was acting like Iain's return wasn't even noteworthy. "Thanks for looking after Dylan."

"No problem," I said automatically. I had to get out of here before I said or did something that I'd regret later.

Iain's hand brushed my bare arm as I went by him. "Jess?" He was frowning at me.

"I have nothing to say to you." I kept my eyes turned away. I had to move.

I wasn't running away I told myself, I had made a tactical retreat.

As I crossed the unit, a small hand touched my arm. "Hello, Jessica." Sister Benjamina looked up at me with her steel grey eyes. "I heard Lasha Cooper is here with her son. Is there anything I can do?"

"Yes, there is Sister," I swallowed and breathed deep. "Dylan is going to be going through some tests. Lasha is in the ER waiting room and a bit upset."

"I'll go see if she needs anything." Sister Ben gave me one of her radiant smiles before she patted my arm and turned toward the door.

Doctor Hector chose that moment to come back through the doors from Medical Imaging that housed the MIR, X-ray, and CT scan sections. I joined him and we made our way back to Dylan's side.

I shoved my hands in my scrub pockets as I realized I was rubbing the arm where Iain had touched me. I had to focus on Dylan right now. He was the priority.

Hell Cat

Will Conall sat at a shadowy table in the far corner of the bar with his back to the wall. He was nursing a drink and watching my every move.

I could feel his dark eyes on me even though I hadn't looked at him in over an hour. I could detect his scent and it tantalized me, making me extraordinarily aware of him. It also made me think about the last time we were together, and I had to squash that thought without mercy. I had a job to do.

There was no way I was going to avoid having a conversation with Will. The more I thought about it, the more I welcomed the idea. I was glad he had found me. Maybe we'd finally get a chance to clear the air. Possibly, we could save our professional relationship, if not our personal one. Although, I knew I would have preferred the latter.

Most of the Kicking Horse's patrons didn't notice the tall dark-haired man in the corner. He wore snug jeans and a black T-shirt that hugged his hard, lean body, and over it all, he wore a black leather coat. I knew that under the clothes his arms and chest were scarred, but he was fit and well-muscled.

I had run my fingertips over that hard body. I still remembered the texture of his skin and the heat that burned within me as we lay side by side, skin touching.

The clothing did help to conceal him, but Will had a talent for making people ignore him. Eyes seem to slide right off of him. I couldn't really explain how it worked, but it did. Mine didn't. I could see Will quite clearly, but then I was a shapeshifter and we had excellent eyesight.

"Get your head back in the game, Helly," I muttered to myself.

I kept the beer and hard stuff coming for the waitresses at the Kicking Horse. It was a rougher than average watering hole in an industrial section of Edmonton.

Jimmy was the bar manager and my current boss. He kept the guys sitting at the long wooden bar lubricated while he pretended to clean the scarred surface.

The majority of our clientele were males. I avoided serving the regulars sitting at the bar as much as possible—to avoid unwanted attention and the need to break any bones. Many of these guys were old enough to be my father, and that alone made me cringe. Some were too young to bother with and I was pretty sure most of them didn't own a mirror.

There was also the fact that, in the late evening, a few of them would try and tap out the Breathalyzer machine. It was a game they played to see who was the drunkest. Now there's a recommendation for you.

I used my Aunt Rita's line on most of them at one time or another. "I don't shit where I eat." It made them laugh and also let them know I wasn't interested. Words could be powerful weapons when used correctly.

I listened to them and collected rumors about the bar robberies that happened before I got here. I sorted information from their conversations. Some of what they said was even useful.

"Hey, Alice," Belinda slumped against the bar, plunking her damp cork bottom tray down next to her.

I used Alice Munro as my name for this contract. Nobody at the bar asked if I was the Nobel laureate for literature, but then I hadn't expected anyone to.

Belinda's breasts were bulging out of her V-neck tank top with the aid of an industrial-strength push-up bra. Her tiny denim shorts were riding up her ass showing a considerable amount of cheek. Belinda was well tipped for her efforts. Her brassy blonde hair with the odd splash of green and too much makeup took most of the attention, and thus the heat, off me. My natural blonde hair looked washed out in the dim lighting, but Belinda blazed, and I was good with that.

Jimmy didn't have a dress code. The waitresses decided on their own how much harassment they wanted, versus how high they expected their tips to be.

I stuck to jeans and T-shirts and, with my assets, I did okay. Especially if the looks I was getting from Will across the room were anything to go by. It was all for appearances anyway, I wasn't here for the tips.

"Hey, Belinda, what do you need?" I gave her a commiserating smile. We only had another forty-five minutes to go and we could close down for the night.

"Fifteen minutes to last call and table six wants a dozen tequila shots and two pitchers of Purple Plank."

"Purple Plank?" I asked to make sure I had heard her right. "Nobody likes it." That was an understatement. It was one step below swill. It was the cheapest draft beer you could get. I had looked it up.

"I know, Jimmy isn't going to re-order it, we're supposed to get rid of it as fast as we can." Belinda pushed bright green bangs out of her eyes. "I told them there was a discount on it tonight. You know, like the featured beer? Not to worry, they aren't too choosey and probably can't taste much right now anyway. Most of them are having trouble standing."

"Ah, smart." I nodded as I continued pouring out the dozen shots. *I'm afraid I've had too much practice at this.*

I'd hired on as a bartender to investigate the robberies. Unfortunately, since I started, no one from any biker gang had materialized to hold up the place. At least while I was here, the building owner got his rent on time.

I gathered up the shots between my spread fingers and deposited them on her tray. "Do they have a designated driver?"

"They have a van coming for them at closing. Don't worry. I don't want any of these guys on the road when you and I are driving home." Belinda winked at me.

"I appreciate that," I said, filling the second pitcher from the tap.

"That guy in the corner has been keeping tabs on you all night," Belinda commented glancing over her shoulder and looking at Will.

He ignored her completely I noted when I glanced up. His eyes locked on mine for a second, and then I broke the contact.

"Yeah, I know," I said as I took the money she offered me. Jimmy didn't let anyone run a tab. You paid up for each round or you didn't get served.

"Do you know him, or should I have Donny roust him out?" She offered to involve the bar bouncer to protect me as she gathered up her tray. "Or, better yet, let me take care of him," she said as she gave me a sly smile and laughed at her own joke.

"No, it's okay I'm acquainted with him, but thanks for the offer." I smiled at Belinda as I gave her back change for the fifty she had handed me. I was sure it would all be tip money.

"He looks like trouble with those dark eyes and that body." Belinda grinned at me. "I hope he shows you a good time." She turned away to head back to deliver the order.

I didn't have time to comment. Sindy was waiting for her order to be filled, and I knew Mattie would be back shortly, too.

"Last call!" Jimmy's bellow cut through the country western music and conversation like a hot knife through butter.

After I placed the pitcher of beer on Mattie's tray and added two rum and Cokes to Sindy's, I could feel eyes on me, so I glanced over at the bar manager.

Jimmy gave me a wordless frown from his end of the bar and tipped his whiskered covered chin at Will in the corner. I was touched that our grizzled, grouchy old boss was concerned that Will was eyeing me.

I shook my head and gave Jimmy a thumbs-up. He narrowed his eyes at me but, as usual, didn't say anything. Jimmy was a man of few words.

I returned to my section of the bar and did a fast cleanup of the surfaces before Belinda made a return trip with one more order. I still had a beer keg to change out too.

*****

Will Conall took a shallow sip of the room temperature Glenlivet from the short glass. He'd been slowly turning the tumbler between his hands for the past few hours. It was a younger whisky than he usually drank, but it was the only thing the bar served by way of a decent brand.

His server Sindy, ambled over again as she had every half hour.

"Can I get you anything else?" she leaned on the table, giving him a good look at her considerable cleavage. She cocked one hip so her painted on jeans tightened. The girl was pretty enough with her fuchsia pink hair and her heavily made up dark brown eyes, but Will didn't care.

"No thanks, I'm good," he said, shaking his head and turning his eyes back to the lean, hard-bodied blonde behind the bar.

"Okay." Sindy looked him over one more time, gave a little sigh, and moved on.

There was only one woman in this establishment Will was interested in. When her charade of a job was done for the evening, he would corner Helly Cooper.

Helly had only looked up at him three times all night, and each time those blue eyes rested on him, he'd felt them strike him right in the heart.

Her expression had remained blank when she saw him. No reaction at all. Like looking at him was the same as looking at one of the grubby oil-patch workers. She hadn't given him any sign of recognition. She'd acted like she could have cared less that he had been sitting here since nine o'clock, waiting for her.

Stupidly, he had hoped for some emotion. Whether Helly had intended it or not her attitude had gotten under his skin. They had known each other a long time, but Helly was a cool one. She always had been.

Will had stopped being angry with her months ago. He had to admit he had driven her away. She hadn't cut all her ties to him and Security and Protection Services on a whim. It was his fault, even though admitting it to himself still stuck in his throat.

He had to concede he was the one who had crossed the line. It was past time to do something about it if he was ever going to get her to come back to the company.

He had reconciled himself to the fact that he couldn't be with Helly, not like she wanted. He couldn't, not with his issues, but they could still work together and, for him, that would be enough.

***

We got through last call and Donny only had to pour two people into cabs. No one argued with big Donny.

True to their word, table six had a van pick them up. It was nice to see people were occasionally doing the smart thing. I figured they must be from one of the bigger drilling companies.

Horizontal drilling was the new hot technology for oil and gas companies. The technology allowed access to pockets of the resource previously too expensive to go after. Now that the price of oil had gone back up, Edmonton was back to feeling like a boom town. The Kicking Horse patrons had the disposable income to prove it. I knew Jimmy pulled in several thousand each night, a tidy sum for a dump like this.

By the time I had finished running all the dishes through the dishwasher and stacked the trays of glasses, the bar was almost empty.

Jimmy was cashing out and shoving wads of bills into the deposit bag. The rest the staff were cleaning up and wiping down the tables. I was faster than usual at this task because I wanted to get out on time. I wanted to get Will out of here. Why had he felt it was necessary to sit for hours scrutinizing me while I poured drinks? He hadn't come up to the bar and tried to talk to me. He could have left me a number to call him later, but maybe he thought he'd lose me again. He had to know I had been expecting him to track me down for the past couple of weeks. I had stopped covering my tracks as well as I had in the beginning. I was getting tired of being alone.

I hadn't seen Will in over ten months, and we hadn't parted on the greatest of terms.

I knew he wasn't comfortable working with me anymore, so it had been time for me to move on. I left SPS after working for them for almost nine years and hadn't been in contact with him or the company since.

That being said, something compelling must have made him find me. I knew he wanted to talk to me because he had stayed seated at his table as I worked my way over to him. I glanced over at him now, and we exchanged a watchful look.

He was waiting. Like a predator stalking his prey.

Every time I met his dark eyes, I felt something. It was hard to describe, but even after ten months I still had feelings for that man.

I was spraying cleaner on a worn table top when the front door of the bar slammed open, hitting the wall.

I cut my eyes to the entrance.

Three men walked in wearing dark windbreakers, dark jeans, and ski masks, each carrying a weapon. The last one across the threshold paused by the door to close it and to throw the dead bolt.

Donny was still outside.

From the corner of my eye, I saw Will get quietly to his feet.

"Nobody moves," ordered the male leading the three new arrivals. He was wearing a navy windbreaker with a splash of white paint on the sleeve. He raised his pistol in a one-handed grip and walked up to the bar, no doubt trusting the hand gun would freeze us where we stood. He leveled the pistol right at Jimmy's face. "Hand over the cash and keep your hands on the bar."

He couldn't know about the shotgun Jimmy kept loaded under the bar. Probably it was just as well, if Jimmy went for the rifle, Jimmy would be dead.

The taller guy at the door swung a rifle up and pointed it at the waitresses. *Who brings a hunting rifle to a robbery?*

"Get over to the wall," he growled at them.

They scurried to the wall by the kitchen doors and froze like deer in the headlights. Each one of them clutched a tray of dirty glasses like it was a shield.

The third guy advanced farther into the room and held a rifle as well. He didn't have it braced correctly against his body and waved it around like an idiot. He clearly wasn't sure who he should cover—me or the two old guys to the left of Jimmy still seated at the bar.

At least Jimmy's cronies were following the bar manager's example. They each kept one hand flat on the bar and had a death grip on their beer mugs with the other. They weren't moving, but their eyes were bulging pretty good. To these thieves, it must have looked like a nearly empty bar with a few old guys and some women.

Easy pickings?

That almost made me smile. They hadn't counted on me or Will. They certainly didn't look like members of a biker gang, so this had to be something else.

I knew Will would take out the guy at the door first. I would have to go for whoever seemed like the most imminent threat. I was almost equidistant between the leader and his idiot sidekick. I watched both of them carefully. With my shapeshifter abilities, I would be on my target before he knew it.

I could move faster than standard humans, not faster than a bullet, but close. We shapeshifters considered ourselves human too. But we were enhanced, where regular or standard humans were not.

None of the gunmen had noticed Will. I could pick him out by the back wall in the gloomy light. He made his way effortlessly across the room to the door. He soundlessly skirted the tables and chairs and got behind his target.

Will moved quickly and efficiently as he grabbed the guy by the door. He wrapped his arm around the guy's neck and squeezed off his air. Will grabbed the rifle with his other hand as he eased the gunman down to the floor with almost no noise.

It was a practiced move, and Will did it fluidly. Had I been facing the opposite way, like the others, I wouldn't have known anything was going on either. One down, two to go.

I turned my body toward my target as I prepared to make my move, now that we were down to two. I would take the guy at the bar because he was their leader. *Cut the head off the snake so to speak.*

Idiot here, waved his weapon between me and the bar regulars. If I took out the leader, this guy would probably fold without a fuss.

The kitchen door swung open and Juanita, Jimmy's wife and the bar cook, shuffled into the room. She was completely unaware we were in the midst of a robbery.

Idiot was startled and swung his weapon toward Juanita. He fired his rifle at her. Everyone snapped their heads in his direction.

Juanita shrieked, the waitresses screamed and dropped their trays. Juanita threw her arms over her head, turned tail, and ran back into the kitchen. Thank God the shot went wide and hit one of the wooden posts, splintering it.

With the commotion, I changed direction. I ran toward the idiot and, before he could turn on me, I grabbed the gun stock and pushed the barrel up and away from everyone. Then I pulled him into me, easily landing a punch to his throat.

He gagged, his throat was constricted. I pulled the weapon out of his hands and swung the rifle at him. I cracked him in the jaw with the butt, effectively shutting out his lights.

He dropped to the floor as well. I flipped the gun around and pointed it at the leader. Will had beaten me to him. The leader of this ragtag crew was lying unconscious on the floor at Will's feet. I dropped the barrel down and away from Will.

He flicked one eyebrow up at me before he returned his attention to the weapon in his hand. He ejected the clip from the pistol, checked the breach to make sure it was clear, and then laid the pistol on the bar.

Will had the tall guy's rifle that, from here, looked like a Remington 700. He cradled it in the crook of his arm as he leaned down and pulled the balaclava off the robber's face.

Will's eyes met mine, and he gave me a slight shake of his head. No one we knew. Which meant the leader wasn't on any list SPS would have been aware of such as a Canada-wide warrants. He was probably a local.

Will straightened and turned to Jimmy. "Call nine-one-one," he ordered the stunned bar manager.

In the four weeks I'd worked at the bar, I had never seen a look like that on Jimmy's face, he was at a loss for words. Yeah, seeing Will work would do that to you.

"Jimmy?" I prompted to get him moving.

"Yeah, I'm calling." Jimmy growled and reached for the phone under the bar as he aimed a scowl first at Will then at me. I ignored him and turned back to Will.

"I'll go check on the bouncer," Will said. "Have you got this?"

"Yeah, all good," I said. I flicked my eyes over to Mattie, Belinda, and Sindy. "One of you, go to the kitchen and check on Juanita," I ordered.

All three scurried into the kitchen. They paused only briefly to avoid the broken glass and trays in their path. I couldn't blame them for being scared, but the danger was over.

One handed, I flipped my assailant on to his stomach. His weight was nothing to me. I nudged his hands away from his sides with my booted foot. I needed to keep an eye on all three of the gunmen while Will was outside.

My old boss wouldn't have asked for the police if he had killed the guy by the door. There was no smell of death either. If he had, we would be calling SPS for a cleanup crew. They would handle the body and scrub the vicinity.

The front door swung open again and Will had his shoulder braced under the big bouncer's armpit. He helped Donny through the door and down onto a chair.

"Did he get shot?" I asked, looking at the blood running down Donny's forehead.

"No, he took a blow to the head," Will said, steadying Donny so he wouldn't slide out of the chair.

"Belinda!" I yelled to the kitchen. "Donny needs the first aid kit."

Will returned to the entrance and grabbed the tallest gunmen's left ankle. He dragged him over to where the idiot was laying prone next to me. I rolled him onto his stomach as well. This was so that, if any of them regained consciousness and were sick, they wouldn't choke.

He also dragged the leader over to the other two thieves, again by his ankle, to complete the set, and I flipped him over too.

It was Juanita who came bustling out of the kitchen, carrying a first aid kit and apparently unhurt. She called over to Jimmy and he waved her off dismissively. So she turned to Donny and began fussing over the bouncer.

I frowned. Juanita seemed to have regained her equilibrium remarkably quick.

Jimmy was on the phone with emergency services dispatch, explaining what had just gone down. He rolled his eyes at me as he listened to the dispatcher's instructions.

I leaned down and removed the ski masks from the other two guys. I lifted their heads by their hair to get a good look at their faces. Nope, nobody I recognized. Well, that sucked.

"Have you got cuffs?" Will asked as he gave them a cursory look as well.

"I have riot cuffs." Will had the Remington in his hand and the Ruger now lodged in his belt at the small of his back.

So I dropped the Winchester's barrel to point at the floor. "Give me a second to get them."

I walked behind the bar and dug my shoulder bag out. I extracted the white plastic restraining cuffs. The cops could trade the plastic cuffs for real ones at their leisure.

Both of the regulars left at the bar took the opportunity to head to the men's room. The older one stumbled a bit as they made for the restroom. His friend grabbed him by the arm to lend support as they wobbled unsteadily out of the room.

"This was amateur hour," Will said quietly as he drew each man's hands behind their back and I secured their wrists.

"Yeah, when they walked in, I was hoping we would nail someone from a biker gang tonight. Maybe we should see if we can get anything out of navy windbreaker here."

The former leader of the awesome trio was making groaning sounds. He had a serious bruise on his jaw were Will had clipped him.

I went through his pockets. "No wallet or ID," I commented. That was what I had expected, but I had to look anyway.

I tried idiot's coat pockets and, running true to form, idiot had ID on him. "Percival Jenkins," I said reading his license. The photo matched, but anything could be faked. "Who names their kid Percival?"

Percival was coming around too. He was fairly young, maybe eighteen. The other two were older, between twenty and twenty-five.

All three had average builds with Percival on the skinnier side. They had medium brown hair and unremarkable features. Upon closer inspection I could tell the clothing was cheap, worn, and several years out of date. Possibly from a thrift store.

"Are you seeing what I'm seeing?" Will asked.

"I think so," I said.

Will leaned close to Percival's ear and said in a low tone, "Hey, Percy, what's your big brother's name?"

"Alvin or Marvin?" Percival asked. His voice was hoarse and groggy as his eyelids fluttered.

Will and I shared a grin.

"I need ice for Donny, *cosa dulce*," Juanita called over to me as she cleaned up Donny. The bouncer hung his head and hadn't moved from his seat.

I raised an eyebrow at Will. "Is Juanita talking to you, sweet thing?"

"Funny," Will said dryly, even though there was humor in his whisky-colored eyes. It had felt good to work together again. I had missed this.

I left Will to keep an eye on the idiot squad. He was going through the third guy's pockets as I went behind the bar. I found a clean towel, dampened it slightly, and added a scoopful of ice.

"Who's that guy?" Jimmy asked me as I replaced the scoop in the ice bin.

I knew who he meant so there was no point in pretending. "He's a friend of mine. He does security." Will was much more than that, and so was I, but I didn't think it was necessary to give Jimmy all the details. Will certainly wouldn't thank me for it.

Jimmy grunted at my answer as I brushed a strand of blonde hair off my cheek. The hair must have been dislodged from my pony tail when I took out Idiot Boy.

I looked steadily back at Jimmy, but he didn't say anything about Will, even though I could see he wasn't happy. Instead, he changed the focus to me. "That was some punch, Alice. You have some experience taking guys down?" It wasn't really a question and I had already tipped my hand.

"Some," I said. My expression told him that was all he was getting out of me.

"Yeah, I'm still here," Jimmy said into the phone, but his eyes bored into me.

Dispatch wouldn't let him off the line until the uniforms got here. I raised my eyebrows at Jimmy. He shook his head and turned his back on me. I took it our conversation was over. I headed back around the bar to take Juanita the iced towel for Donny.

The idiot squad were all sitting up, though still on the floor with Will standing to one side and keeping an eye on them. All three looked embarrassed, and scared, I noted as I passed them.

I handed Juanita the towel, and she gently placed it on the left side of Donny's head, where his bald patch started, covering the swelling.

Flashing blue and red lights hit the window. "Cops are here!" Sindy called from the kitchen.

Trusting the Wolf

I woke with a start, my heart pounding like a jackhammer. The taste of blood coated the back of my throat, a ghost of a memory. I'd killed Geoff, again.

With the sheet clenched in my fists, I struggled to get my heart rate under control. I didn't need a mirror to tell me gold rolled over my shapeshifter eyes.

The rage, fear, and revulsion faded slowly as I came back to myself. Wearily, I rubbed my face.

This was getting old.

"Get a grip, Lottie," I told myself irritably and flung back the covers.

Geoff was a member of my pack and used to run security with me. I never much liked him. We didn't get along, but we could work together.

Our alphas discovered the beta wolf murdered one of our pack members and poisoned another. I didn't know anything about it until it was too late.

How did I miss the signs pointing to his guilt? *I'm a security screw up, that's how.*

The need to be outside overwhelmed me. I didn't bother to grab a robe before leaving the bedroom.

My feet unerringly took me through the dark house. From the kitchen, I exited by the back door and stepped into the walled-in back garden. The cooler night air helped and I breathed in deep. Slowly, my blood pressure dropped, but it wasn't enough. Usually, when I was surrounded by growing things, I could unwind. Not tonight.

In daylight, the yard was a multi-hued display. After dark, the plants released their complex scents into the still night air. Surrounded by the rich, spicy perfumes, I breathed them in again, hoping to calm down. But still it wasn't enough.

Abruptly, I opened the outside shower door. The metal spring protested with a squawk, but I was the only one to hear it.

Even though the new moon had yet to rise, the interior was clearly defined as my wolf sight took over. The teak floor, smooth under my bare feet, felt cold. My landlord salvaged the wood from a sailboat cockpit to build it. The wooden grid allowed the water from the rainspout shower head to pass through to the drainage system and water the plants. We experienced droughts more often now on the Island, and Guy Tremblay was the plan ahead type.

A bath puff and towel hung from the row of brass hooks, but I wasn't there to shower, at least not yet. I hug my panties and tank top from an empty hook.

At five-foot, ten inches, I carried a respectable amount of muscle. With my well-developed arms extended over my head I reached for the night sky. I bent forward and placed my hands flat on the wooden floor, and felt my hamstrings stretch. None of this naked yoga was strictly necessary, but it loosened up my limbs. I felt a consuming need to shift and burn off the nightmare hangover with a run.

As I straightened, brief bloody images flashed in my head. Geoff managed to kill and terrorize his way from Campbell River to the Cowichan Valley before we made him pay. It didn't matter that he deserved to die, I just wished I could escape the images.

I remember every detail of Geoff's death with excruciating clarity. The feel of his flesh as it gave way under my teeth, the hot spurt of his blood in my mouth and on my face. My anger, fear, and the taste of bile, along with the rank smell of his fur. A shiver of revulsion passed through me and made me want to puke.

Instead, I shook off the overpowering feelings, took one more deep, calming breath, and my barriers dropped.

Pure, clean power washed through me, as I open myself up to the pool of magic that resided inside my human shape. The magic cleaned and transformed my spirit as it reshaped my body. The power drove away the suffocating feelings of guilt and released my wolf.

I held a considerable amount of magic and my transformation was always swift and easy. As a result, I stood on four large wolf paws and lifted my head to shake out my sable-brown coat.

My world was sharper and more distinct in my wolf form. Images hidden by the night come in to focus. Smells were sharper, like the tang of small animals, the remnants of my neighbor's barbeque last night, and the green smells of plants around me made my nose twitch. Each sound was crisper and clearer too. Everything was less complicated in this shape. I loved my wolf, she was my release.

With my head and shoulders I pushed the double-hinged door open, and loped across the yard. There is a gate with a loop of rope attached to the latch, but it's fiddly. Besides, it was nothing for me to clear the six-foot stone wall, and I couldn't wait. I wanted to run, I needed to run.

I was over the fence in a heartbeat and landed with barely a sound. My claws dug into the soft dirt and dried grass, and bit deep into the turf. I gathered my hindquarters under me and thrust forward into the night.

When I ran in my animal shape it always made me feel better. With no reservations, I gave myself over to my wolf completely.

Given the reins, she consumed me and escaped the horrible guilt the dreams always invoked. I didn't regret killing Geoff. He brought his death onto himself. What I did regret was I never questioned his behavior. My dislike for him blinded me. I was supposed to be an impartial investigator, in any given situation. Not a great recommendation for a security supervisor, charged with keeping the pack safe.

My paws hit the soft dirt in a steady rhythm and fresh air filled my lungs.

The night creatures froze in place as I passed by. I didn't care, I wasn't hunting. Instead, I dropped my head, laid my ears back, and pushed myself harder. Building speed to take the next ridge, and I instinctively head for pack lands and leave my neighbourhood behind.

The Vancouver Island Clan, my pack, hadn't yet announced its presence to the world. Although I knew my alpha, Iain was gearing up for this scary step. Until then, I needed to remain unseen.

There were plenty of wolves on Vancouver Island, but not too many here in the Cowichan Valley. I am a shapeshifter wolf, which means I'm larger than a full-blood wolf. One look at me, and there would be panic calls to the conservation office or the cops.

Alone, in the wee hours of the morning, with no one to look out for, but myself, I skirted the glistening waters of Crofton Lake then turned to the west. A well-used path lay before me. The trail would take me up the backside of Mount Richards.

I threaded my way through the immense big-leaf maples and Douglas-fir. My wolf sight allowed me to easily slip in, out, and over obstacles. Between Sitka spruce, and arbutus trees, over deadfalls of cedar and a clump of wild blackberry bushes before silently landing on the track again.

The exertion took over all my conscious thought. The rush of blood through my veins invigorated me. Encouraged, I stretched myself out to run harder. I welcomed the cool breeze as it ran over my muzzle and combed gentle fingers through my fur.

As I entered the pack's farmland, I felt the strong tug of magical wards. The familiar pull of our land, our territory, and my pack. I turned right, and took the path leading down to the gun range.

The faint, yet sharp smell of cordite hung in the air from target shooting a day ago. The whole idea of using weapons was still felt foreign to me.

After we saw how silver rounds worked on the deadly menace Geoff became, we setup the range. The pack security team and I obtained our firearms acquisition permits. Once we possessed the right paperwork, target practice began, and it turned out I wasn't a bad shot. If it were only for hunting with a rifle, it would be fine, but the alphas and I recognized we needed to step up our game.

We now know there are dangerous, otherworldly things we need to protect our pack from. Things which required more than claws, teeth, and cunning.

"You can never ignore a threat," Ben Case said.

Our farm manager was right. If it happened once, it could happen again. The cave on Mount Tzouhalem contained only one of these dangers.

To achieve our goals, my team required serious and intensive training. Both to understand how to deal with any future threats and to teach the skills to other pack members.

How could I supervise the security team if I was having doubts about my ability? I needed to get over what happened with Geoff and get on with the job, for everyone's safety.

A left turn brought me to the target butts. I ran along the fifty feet from the butts to the firing point, setup and ready for the start of training tomorrow.

As I traveled the length of the tree-lined range I dropped down to a trot. When I came out from behind the observation post, the slight breeze was behind me. I leapt over the barricades and landed with my nose pointing north. That was when I caught an unfamiliar scent on the night air.

A huge, coal-black wolf stepped out of the shadows from a copse of trees, not twenty feet away.

I stopped dead and stared hard at him. A growl rippled out of my throat. The strange wolf startled me a bit, but I maintained control of myself and didn't automatically lunge at him.

His golden eyes glinted back at me as he watched me silently.

I drop my head and bared my teeth as another deep growl emitted from my thick timber wolf throat. Instinctively, my hackles rose as his musk drifted over to me, invading my nose. He was not pack. *He isn't one of mine, and he is in my territory.*

I charged.

It didn't matter to me the male was bigger, broader, or more heavily muscled. I slammed into him and knocked him back a foot.

My claws dug in, I spun around, and ran at him again. I slammed into him harder, and this time he went down. I knew he let me knock him to the ground, but unless he planned to challenge me, he had to submit, and it was my right to make him.

The big black beast folded his legs and rolled onto his belly. His jaws parted and he flashed his teeth, like he was laughing at me. The male stretched out to his full length, and rolled onto his back, with his tongue lulling, and exposed his underside to me.

I narrowed my eyes at this insolent ass insulting me. He would regret not taking me seriously. Muscles coiled, I sprang, and landed on top of him with a snarl. I grabbed his throat between my teeth. I gripped the flesh harder than was necessary as my claws sank into his hide. He stiffened as his mood abruptly sobered.

A long, deep warning emitted from low in my throat. I put all my pent up emotions into it as I kept up the pressure and waited. He stilled completely, it was his choice, and he knew I was serious. Finally, he whined an acceptance.

With a last growl, I released his throat and stepped off him.

The wolf shifted into his human form and he slowly stood, rubbing at his corded neck. "You play rough." His tone mocked me as his smile widen.

From the burgeoning moon, it was clear he was a large man, over six feet with a broad chest, and powerful arms. I couldn't make out the shade of his eyes in the dim light, but I could see the sparkle of mirth in their depths. His riot of red hair stood out from his head with a matching beard brushing his broad hairy chest. I tracked a line of darker hair down his body, but cut my examination short of the goods. I didn't want to be distracted. Even in his human shape, the male looked wild.

My magic drained away as I shifted back into my human form.

A few feet back from the male, I stood on human legs. The distance would give me a chance to react if I were forced to kick the crap out of him in my human shape or shift to my wolf.

"Who are you and what are you doing on VIC pack land?" I demanded.

"Being accosted by a beautiful she-wolf, apparently," he said in a cheerful, pleasant tone, clearly enjoying himself. He spread his hands to show he offered me no harm, but there were all kinds of dangerous. I didn't know this wolf, I couldn't trust him.

His light accent tickled my ear, but I couldn't identify its origin. His grin stayed in place as he cautiously stepped toward me.

I couldn't back away. I couldn't act submissive and let him see he intimidated me. It was an alpha wolf thing. I didn't run our pack, but I held a position that demanded respect and, by God, this wolf would comply.

The male's closer proximity allowed me to inhale his scent. His aroma made me want to breathe in deep, he smelled amazing. His scent waged war on me and I struggled to control my wolf. She wanted to be let loose, but I pushed her urging aside. *I must maintain control.*

"Answer the question," I bit out. My anger—mostly directed at myself for my reaction—dripped from my word, but I couldn't help it. My lack of control bothered me even more.

"Absolutely, my dove." He took another slow step forward. Deliberately, he closed the distance between us. "I'm Zavier Koering, I work for SPS. I'm here to teach your weapons course." He watched me intently, like he knew my deepest secrets and merely waited for me to confirm them. "I'm a friend of Will Conall and Helly Cooper. But you, my dove, you may call me Zav." His eyes traveled over me suggestively and he missed nothing.

Heat bloomed in my checks at his intense scrutiny. "I am not your 'dove.'" *Whatever that meant.* "You weren't supposed to be here until tomorrow morning," I said tersely. "And stop staring. Shapeshifters usually show better manners."

"You are so beautiful, I can't help myself. And I am not like most shapeshifters."

How did I know he would say that?

He took another step forward.

"It's abundantly obvious you're not," I said dryly and as the words left my mouth, I wanted to bite them back.

"I'm glad you agree." Koering's chuckle, self-satisfied and he paced closer still.

"What are you doing out here in the middle of the night?" I diverted the conversation, hanging on to my patience by a mere thread.

"I am checking out the lay of the land and the facilities before I start the course tomorrow." He arched one copper eyebrow at me as he came to stand directly in front of me. "What's your name?"

"Lottie Fistbinder, head of pack security." I folded my arms across my chest and used my best glower on him.

"Ah, I hoped you might be. It is an immense pleasure to meet you." If anything, his smile grew more wolfish. "Lottie is short for Charlotte? Yes?" He stood only inches away from me now, and I could feel the heat radiating off his skin. His scent surrounded me. I'd never encountered a male who smelled this tantalizing in my life.

Uh oh. My wolf pushed against my consciousness, but I ignored her. In a situation like this, it was more important for my brain to stay in charge and run this exchange, not my instinct and hormones.

"Yes, but everyone calls me Lottie."

"Must I remind you, I am not everyone?" Koering's lips parted in a flash of white teeth. He slowly raised his right hand, as his eyes locked on mine. Koering's open hand inched slowly toward me. He ran one finger over my skin, along my collarbone to my shoulder.

The shock of his touch and the feelings the contact triggered made me jump back. "Keep your hands to yourself unless invited."

"But will you, Charlotte? Will you invite me?"

"Depends," I said as I narrowed my eyes and blatantly looked him up and down. I could see he relaxed his guard, confident of his effect on me, conceited even.

I lashed out with my right foot and swept his feet out from under him, he never saw it coming.

Koering landed hard on his butt. Dust and the fragrance of crushed vegetation filled the air.

I looked down at him with one eyebrow raised. "It depends on whether you respect me or not."

For his part, Koering frowned up at me from his seat on the crushed ferns. "Charlotte, of course, I respect you, I could never mate a woman I didn't respect."

My jaw dropped as I blinked in shock at his words. Weirdly, he sounded sincere. What was it with this guy?

"What are you talking about?" I finally managed to get out.

Instead of words, he replied with a lunge at me. Before I could react, he grabbed my leg behind my right knee and the leg collapsed. I staggered forward and Koering pulled me down on top of him.

Skin to skin.

I inhaled to respond to this attack, but before I could snarl one word at him. His firm, warm lips covered mine and he rolled us over, his larger frame pressed me into the bed of ferns.

Caught off guard, my wolf took over. Maybe because I'd never experienced attention from a male like this—ever.

Lips parting, I clutched his broad shoulders, and I allowed this strange, attractive man to kiss me. And heaven help me, I kissed him right back.

Sensations I'd never experienced before flooded through me. His hot mouth made my lips part farther, and allowed his tongue to tease mine. He tasted incredible.

Koering broke the kiss after several moments of heated contact. His chest pressed against my breasts, as out of breath and excited as I was. The movement caused all sorts of interesting sensations to course through me.

His lips curved into a smug, knowing smile. "Say you want me, my dove," he teased arrogantly. And his arrogant words killed it.

Excited by his scent and the physical contact of his body my wolf wanted to submit. His kiss and the touch of his hands on my skin stirred things I never knew I could feel. I was so tempted to let the sensation take me over, to give in completely.

I'd experienced my share of play, but nothing made me feel even remotely close to this before, and I felt a tumble of emotions—fear, desire, and a touch of annoyance. My human side needed to be the side which ruled me. Anger flared and I couldn't help what came out of my mouth.

"What I would say, is this attitude is an abuse of authority on your part." I tried to sound cool and detached but in truth, I was burning up with a combination of anger, frustration, and reaction. "You'll be leading the instruction and exercises tomorrow, in a position of authority? Misuse of power isn't something we tolerate here, in our pack."

His eyes opened wider in surprise. I guess this wasn't the usual response he got. He swiftly climbed to his feet and leaned down to offer me a hand. When I took it, his fingers closed over mine and the contact felt unbelievably right. I really needed to get a grip on myself.

"This is true, my beauty," Zavier nodded with a slight smile. He trailed his fingertips down my neck causing me to shiver. "But it doesn't change the fact you will be my mate."

I started to laugh. Yes, he kissed the begeezus out of me and I liked it. Hey, I was only flesh and blood and magic, but there was a line I couldn't allow him to cross, not without my permission.

"Why are you laughing?" Zavier's frown deepened as I attempted to get myself under control again.

"I know nothing about you beyond what Helly and Will have told me." I put some space between us, for my own good. "You might be a good guy, I don't know. But what I do know is you're trying to overwhelm me. The mating talk is more of the same. Let it drop and we won't say another word about it." There was a clear warning in my tone.

"Are we not shapeshifters? Are we not, at least half of the time, animals?" The way he said the last sentence, with a low timbre in his voice, sparked a reaction in my blood. His tone made my breath come faster, much like his kiss had. But still, this wasn't the time or the place for either of those things.

"I don't know how you do things in your pack, but here on the Island, we strive to let our human side rule us." I said this breathing in and out as slow as possible to get a grip on my wolf. Giving in would be too easy and I wanted what Zav offered, but I couldn't yield and still keep my self-respect.

"Your words say no, but your body and your scent tell me something different." Zav leaned in for another kiss.

"No," I said and gave him a hard stare in my last attempt to get through to the man. Shapeshifters were persistent, especially since we couldn't lie to each other, our scent gave us away. He was right, I wanted him, but allowing it wasn't a good idea. Not when we were required to work together closely. "How would it look to my team if I took up with a wolf I'd just met? While during such an important training course?"

"All right," Zav nodded.

He stepped back, and his expression turned serious. The male turned his back on me for a moment as he breathed deep. I knew he was attempting to get his wolf back under control. Finally, he straightened his spine, turned, and walked stiffly back over to me. This time he stayed a respectful distance from my personal space. I gave him the same hard stare I gave Silas or Ryan when they screwed up.

"Charlotte Fistbinder of the Vancouver Island Clan—" He gave me a formal nod. "I, Zavier Yul Koering, of no pack, apologize for making unwanted advances and laying my hands upon you. I apologize for the liberties I took, please forgive my boldness." His head dipped in a short bow. "If you would like to report me to your alpha, I understand. I will take the consequences."

Okay, that was weird. "No, I don't think reporting you will be necessary."

"You accept my apology?"

"Yes."

"Thank you. You did take me by surprise though."

"You underestimated me. As my alphas would say that was your first mistake."

"True," he lifted his head now and looked at me with a closed, reserved expression. "Your alphas are wise and it's no wonder Will and Helly made a home with your pack." Something flickered in his eyes for a second. But whatever it was, it disappeared too quickly for me to identify the emotion. "Again, I apologize. Would you like to report my misconduct to Will or Helly?" He pressed.

And explain how I'd ended up pinned under a naked male far longer than I should have allowed? No thank you.

"Will there be any more shenanigans during the training course?" I folded my arms over my chest again. This time he kept his eyes locked on my face.

"No, Charlotte, I will be completely professional during the Ex." He dropped his head again in a sincere nod. I got the feeling he wanted to say more but he kept it to himself.

I shook my head at him. I knew it was past time for me to get out of here. "I don't have time for games. I'll be at the main house by seven a.m. I'll see you then. I hope your weapons skills are better than your unarmed combat." I used humour to cover my fluster, and I hoped he wouldn't notice.

His laughter erupted. "Ah, my dove, my skills are vast and highly developed—I hesitate to apply them to such a fragile flower as you. I would never want to hurt you."

It didn't take long for the supercilious Zav to return. And what was with the fragile flower remark?

Wordlessly, I backed away from the man. He thought a lot of himself. Whether his words were hubris or fact, I couldn't continue this conversation, not in the state my emotions were in.

"Have a good evening," I said lamely, before I turned away. Between one stride and another, I flowed into my wolf and ran back down the trail home when I heard his parting words.

"Until tomorrow my dove, safe travels," Zav pitched his words to reach me.

I ran faster.

***

Zav listened to Charlotte leave through the wood as she dashed back along her original route. She hardly made a sound. If he were not a shapeshifter and a trained field operative, he doubted he would have heard her enter the clearing in the first place. He inhaled the last of her scent as he dug his toes into the dirt to further contain his excitement.

Charlotte was magnificent. What wit, strength of character, and humor. Her eyes, so dark brown they appeared black in the dim light, he wanted to immerse himself in their depths. Her eyes reminded him of the Black Sea on a moonless night. He frowned, thinking about how clouded her gaze had been in the beginning, haunted even. His attention sharpened her focus and chased the ghosts away. This made him smile.

He wanted to touch her. Feel her soft, dusky skin of her Métis heritage. To bury his fingers in her ebony-black hair, cut shorter than the pictures he'd initially seen in her file. Her eyes appeared different as well, more serious. The change in appearance caused him to doubt she was the woman who captivated him over a month ago, but only for a moment.

Her strength and opinions fascinated him too, not to mention her use of shifter magic. He loved the fact she'd taken him by surprise. She would keep him on his toes, this one, and his grin widened.

Charlotte might be different from what he'd imagined, but not in a negative way. The strength of her character was complemented by in her strong jawline, the high cheek bones of her face, and of course her words. He enjoyed sparring with her. The witty female gave him as good as he got.

He admitted she'd well and truly put him in his place. He'd deserved it.

The things he'd said, the touching, and the kissing. He knew he was crossing a line when it happened. In some ways, Zav felt grateful Charlotte called him on his behavior before he'd gotten completely out of control. In others ways, he would have liked to see what could have happened.

He admitted to himself he'd been entirely too forward for their first meeting. He'd come close to ruining everything when he allowed his wolf to rule his actions. As soon as he'd spotted the female on the range, and inhaled her scent, his wolf immediately came off the chain.

His lapse in control was a stupid mistake which he sorely regretted. His actions spoke of impulsiveness and immaturity, behaviour he hadn't displayed in a long time. Even so, her scent told him she would be his. No, better to not to think about it yet. Charlotte was no push over.

Time would be required to get her to trust him. She shouldered a considerable amount of responsibility in her pack. She was smart, logical, and no doubt talented according to Will. A cunning wolf and Zav wanted her. This one, she would be his mate—he felt it in his bones.

Tomorrow, right off the top, Zav needed to fix what he'd done and change her opinion of him. He would show Charlotte he wasn't some primitive wolf, or a dominating asshole. He'd do this by showing her the other side of his character, his professional side, and dial back the impulsive wolf. The wolf who wanted to show off for the female and prove his prowess.

Zav's instincts and her scent told him the attraction was mutual. But if she wanted to keep their relationship on a professional foot, he would. Charlotte also didn't strike him as someone who allowed herself to be ruled by her urges. She would be required to learn much over the next few weeks. He would help her, not harass her.

He had to work on growing her trust by watching, listening, and paying attention to how she felt. It was important she respect him in return. How could she love him if she didn't respect him?

After all this time, all these years, he knew she was the one. The one he'd been waiting for his whole life, for his partner, his mate. He would move cautiously or he might blow it with her.

It was time to go. He turned and jogged toward the route he used to travel out to the range, shifting back into his wolf as he went. His movements were fast and well-practiced. He held an immense pool of magic at his disposal as well, being alpha bred. He hadn't been bragging, much, when he told her he possessed skills, in many areas.

Zav's speed increased to a trot as he moved along the firing points. He easily found her scent again as he retraced her route down the line of trees. The wolf paused to look over the target butts and sandbags. One thing kept coming back to him, how fervently she'd responded to his kiss. She *would* be his, and together, they would be explosive.

Then it would take patience and perseverance to get her to leave her pack.

Website http://blackyvy50.wix.com/yvonnerediger
    Facebook http://www.facebook.com/vicshapeshifters/
    Twitter http://www.twitter.com/blackyvy
    Instagram Blackyvy50
    YouTube: https://www.youtube.com/channel/
UCRg1KoOYF0e1nQuhy5rV-wA?

www.ingramcontent.com/pod-product-compliance
Lightning Source LLC
Chambersburg PA
CBHW020311150626
46552CB00022B/2700